Eliza
Stone

by
Jane Weymouth

Acknowledgements
With thanks to my two U3A creative writing groups,
my editor Zoe King and my family.

Contents

Chapter One - Childhood

In the morning, somewhere in the village, a cock crowed. Eliza woke and slid out of bed, moving quietly so as not to wake her little sister, Maudie, sleeping beside her. There was no sound from the other side of the curtain that divided the girls' side of the room from her brothers'. She dressed, pulled on her buttoned boots and went downstairs to the kitchen. She fetched water from the pump outside and put the kettle on to the still glowing range. Her older brothers, William and Charles were already going off to feed the horses and milk the cows at Manor Farm.

As she set the table, her mother came in, still pinning up her hair and started making the porridge.

"Hurry up, Eliza. Get the little ones ready for school. I've got the baby to feed."

Eliza went back upstairs to make sure that the younger children were washed and dressed. After breakfast it was a relief to set off in her blackened boots and white pinafore down the lane to the village with her three younger brothers. On the way, they saw some farm labourers leaning on their cottage doorposts or talking in twos and threes at their garden gates. One muttered as they went by

"It's alright for some. Your father's always got work."

It was true, their father was a skilled mechanical engineer, a traction engine driver. "What's the matter with them- they make me nervous." asked Eliza of her friend Jacob who'd joined them.

"It's a lockout. They joined the Union and the

famer won't have them back."

They all knew it was a bad time for farming. The black years of the 1880s; severe winters, disease and then cheap wheat coming in from America had lowered prices and wages. Already some village men had moved to the towns or emigrated.

Eliza and her brothers arrived at the school and waited in the playground for the bell. School was compulsory for all children. Eliza paid a penny each and they filed in through separate entrances marked Boys and Girls. In the hallway was an artificial wreath under a glass display case with a card from the School. Eliza's eyes filled with tears. She knew it was for the parents of Mary Ann, a ten year old girl in her class, who'd died of Diphtheria. The long room inside was divided into the Babies and older children managed by Miss Carter and her assistant.

They always started with prayers and a hymn. Then Eliza listened intently as Miss Carter read to the class from Samuel Smiles' book entitled "Self Help".

"Ordinary working class people can study and work hard to improve themselves."

Miss Carter came from the world outside their little village and brought the changing spirit of the times with her. She said, "It's not what you have that matters, but what you are. The souls of the poor are as valuable, your hearts as good and your minds as capable of cultivation as those of the rich."

With her own heart and mind glowing with these words, Eliza went up to the teacher's desk to learn tomorrow's lesson so she could teach the little ones. She planned to be a proper teacher herself one day, not just a pupil teacher. Miss Carter was pleased with her

"Well done, Eliza, you're a bright girl and have a great future ahead of you."

So at lunchtime Eliza went happily home for her bread and dripping, as it was washday and her mother needed her to turn the mangle in the yard. Mother was always in a bad mood on Mondays because the laundry took all day and was very hard work. As Eliza came cautiously out into the yard, she saw that her mother had separated the whites from the coloured clothes and was now up to her armpits in soap, scrubbing. She jerked her head at the tub of rinsed clothes and Eliza obediently put them through the mangle one at a time, ready for Mother to hang up to dry on the washing line. Heaven help them if it rained! Garments would be draped around the fire on a clothes horse for days.

She ran all the way back to school. She had missed playtime but got there just in time for the bell. Miss Carter, with her cane in her hand, ready to punish any mistakes, had written some sentences on the blackboard for the children to copy on their slates. However, just then, a massive traction engine entered the village, its iron wheels grinding noisily on the road, puffing out white clouds of steam. The children were very excited and Miss Carter gave up trying to control them. She announced

"You may go outside, children to watch the team go by."

"That's my father!" shouted Eliza, "he's the driver." She was so proud of him.

All too soon, they heard Miss Carter calling "Come

back inside, children, to finish your work."

Eliza still felt elated as she walked home with her brothers after school. And relieved to find the street was empty. Her friend Jacob said "The labourers have gone to the public house for a meeting."

She and her brothers had to collect sow thistle for the large white pig they kept at the end of the garden. The Suffolk countryside was flat, leaving a huge sky above. Red- polled cattle roamed the pasture and she could hear the bells on the large black-faced sheep grazing on the salt marshes. Suffolk Punch horses pulled a plough, their chestnut sides gleaming in the afternoon sun as they patiently plodded along the furrows. The east wind carried the smell of the sea over the heath. The old villagers told Eliza the Danes had pushed their long ships up the estuaries from the North Sea centuries ago. They had come to raid but eventually settled and married local women. The women hereabouts were still called "fair maids of Suffolk", being tall and fair like their Danish ancestors.

When Eliza and her brothers arrived home at the cottage, Mother was sitting with her feet up on a stool. The smell of rabbit pie came from the kitchen. The cottage with its brick and linoleum floor was spotless. Eliza had helped make the rag mats out of scraps of leftover material. There was a table and chairs, two easy chairs and a sofa. On the shelves were mother's ornaments; a pair of china dogs Father had won for her at a fair and blue glass slippers. A pot of red geraniums sat on the window sill.

"Ah, that's better," Mother said, "I've been on my

feet all day - get me a cup of tea, Eliza."

"Mother," said Eliza carrying the cup in carefully, for tea was expensive, "Miss Carter says I could be a teacher like her one day, if I work hard."

"Miss Carter this and Miss Carter that - that's all we hear these days. A teacher! And who's going to pay for it, that's what I want to know? Housework, cooking and childcare - that's what you'll be doing, my girl - same as I did, same as your grandmother and her grandmother. Now get on and peel those potatoes for supper."

Eliza felt crushed. Her future would be a life of drudgery, but she knew it was no use answering her mother back.

"We saw father's traction engine coming through the village." said little Thomas.

"Did you now, my boy?" replied Mother smiling and ruffling his fair curls.

"He mentioned he'd be out this way, going to the Grange to saw some logs for his Lordship."

Later after supper, Eliza sat with her mother by the fire and helped with the darning and mending. She had to do several rows of knitting before she could go out and play hopscotch and skipping with her friends. She asked her mother, "What will happen to those men who got laid off at the farm?"

"Oh, they'll just have to go cap in hand and ask for their jobs back and forget all this Union nonsense. If you don't work you can't eat."

Later on, Eliza had to help get the younger ones off to bed then go up herself. She cried herself to sleep.

In time, word went round that the men had returned

to work, but were reduced to stealing swedes or taking home corn in their pockets because they couldn't feed their families on the low wages. Adverts appeared in the local paper for "Assisted Emigration to America – rich and extensive land available where a labourer might raise himself by hard work to the level of farmer."

Many left the area in wagons passing through the village on their way to take ship bound for the new world. Eliza and the other children came out to wave them goodbye and God bless! They were told the journey would take weeks.

But the routine of life at home continued as usual. On Tuesday the ironing had to be done. Mother got the stove red hot and put several irons on to heat up; she smoothed out the creases in the clothes and hung them around the fire to air. Eliza had to help.

Mother said "Take special care – those are the boys' shirts."

Dried in the clean country air they smelt sweet and fresh to Eliza. She tried to take comfort in everyday things to heal her disappointment. Hope still lived in her young heart.

The boys were wanted to help with bird scaring that day and had to miss school. Rooks, magpies, crows and pigeons swooped down to peck-up the seed in the fields and they had to shout and rattle tins all day to keep them off.

The family next door lived on slices of bread; Eliza had seen them eating kettle broth - bread with hot water added. They were very poor she thought. Sometimes they ran about barefoot. Their grace at meals was,

> O Heavenly Father bless us
> And keep us all alive;
> There are ten of us to dinner
> And food for only five.

"It seems very hard on them, Mother." said Eliza.

"Yes, child, between the Squire, the Church and the Law, the poor don't have much chance. Here, take a bit of this cheese I made this morning to them."

Eliza knew her family was better off than some – Father was an engineer, earning thirty shillings a week as opposed to the ten shillings labourers got, but the gentry were richer than them all; they lived in the great country houses and manors of the area and occasionally swept through the village in open carriages, the ladies in bright-coloured silks and satins, holding up parasols to protect their pale complexions. The village women stopped what they were doing and curtseyed in respect, while men touched their forelocks. Eliza loved to see them and imagined herself in a carriage, wearing a pale blue silk dress trimmed with lace, shading her face with a cream parasol.

On Saturday Eliza took the children outside to play. The baby cried and coughed as she wrapped her up in her shawl and carried her out for an airing. Mother looked over anxiously, as she had already had one baby die in infancy. But Eliza kissed her little face and sang to her while keeping an eye on the others. They spent all day outside and were as tough as little ponies, kicking up their heels on the heath. Eliza took a basket to collect kindling wood after lunch while the baby was having her nap.

The children couldn't wait for father to come home. Eliza missed him all week. On Saturday evening he arrived in his overalls, his face and hands blackened with oil and dust. He hadn't had a proper wash all week, as he lived in the van with the team while working in surrounding farms. He called out

"Sarah, I'm back!"

Mother rushed over to him for a hug and a kiss. The children clustered round him, trying to get his attention. He had a special eye for Eliza. She leaned against him and he put his arm around her. Nobody minded the dirt and sweat. But after a bath and his dinner, he was off down to the public house to spend the evening singing and step-dancing to the accordion with his friends. However, he gave most of his hard earned wages to mother. She was the one who had to manage the family budget.

Eliza helped fill the tin bath with hot water for the childrens' baths. First the cleanest then on up to the dirtiest ones. The next day was Sunday and everyone had to look respectable in their best clothes ready for church. Mother rustled about in her finest dress, smelling of lavender, with a buttonhole of violets; she brushed the elder boys' clothes and plaited Eliza's hair into a golden rope. The children were scrubbed, darned and starched; they used the good soap, put on their blacked boots and set off on their best behaviour to walk to St. Peter's church. Eliza felt very pious as she walked along holding the little ones hands.

As they approached the black flint tower of the church, she could see the carved green man on the south side - the old nature god which the village still depended upon for their wellbeing. Inside, she saw the red and blue stained glass window of children playing musical instruments. Passing the font with its carved stone roses - she was struck once more by how huge the space was. The bells rang out from the gallery above. She glanced up to see the carved angels on the roof beams holding their open books.

Mother ushered the family into the back pew. The front pews were for the Squire and clergy families, the next for the farmers, then their servants and at the back, the villagers. Eliza loved these times when they were all together, singing hymns at the top of their voices. She knelt down and prayed hard to God for a better life. But it was hard to stay awake in the sermon. The rector would lecture them in his song-song voice, "Respect your employers and be content with your place in life. It is a sin to be envious or angry." Then he announced the next hymn "All things bright and beautiful". They all stood to sing,

> The rich man in his castle
> The poor man at the gate,
> He made them high or lowly
> And ordered their estate"

They went home to the best dinner of the week - Charles said a cheeky grace,

> "God bless the squire and his relations,

And help us know our proper stations."

The children sniggered as they ate meat stew followed by apple pie. Mother frowned at them and said to her husband

"Henry, you and your machines are taking the bread out of the labourers' mouths. Our William can't get work now they don't need so many horses on the farm."

"Now, Sarah, you can't stop progress - mechanisation is the way forward for agriculture. Many have gone to the towns and done well running coffee houses, shops and such. But I will take Will on to work with me, to train him up on the engine." Afterwards Eliza took the children to the small tin Wesleyan Methodist Chapel while father read his newspaper. She liked to hear the lay preacher, for he was a working man like them and spoke of God's kindness and love for the poor. He said in conclusion, "Now we have time for one more hymn before we go and feed the cattle."

Sunday tea was a treat - they had bread with butter or jam and cake.

Once a year, the pig was killed and the hams sent to be smoked in the village at the wheelwright's smoky house, where they hung up under a fire of woodchips and sawdust. The meat would help feed them through the winter. Eliza wasn't allowed to go there because it was thought that women of menstrual age might turn the ham bad. When it got dark, they lit candles made of mutton fat. Eliza wrinkled her nose at the smell of burning fat and the smokiness of the house in the evening.

The weather was getting colder and soon it would be Christmas. Mother brewed some beer. The largest part went to father. As mother said, "He deserves it – he's a good man, he works, without his wages we'd all starve."

The rector put up a tree at the school and Eliza and the children made decorations for it. He smiled sentimentally as the children sang carols. Then he scattered nuts on the floor and the children scrambled for them. At the rectory party Eliza enjoyed playing postman's knock and eating jelly and blancmange. There were presents for them all on the tree. Eliza was pleased with her packet of hair ribbons. She saved the money she got for running errands for the teacher and neighbours, most of which she gave to mother, for a wooden doll for Maudie, her little sister.

Father had made Maudie a wooden cot. In her stocking, Eliza was thrilled to find an orange, apple, and a sugar mouse. The farmers let the men have a day off, an ox was killed and father was given a joint of beef, which they ate with suet pudding dotted with raisins. After the Christmas service. She helped to hang holly and ivy from the ceiling and father uncorked a bottle of his home made wine. Eliza was sad that most of the neighbours' children didn't have stockings or presents.

The first Saturday in January, Eliza joined the rest of the village to see the Hunt meet on the village green outside the old inn. The huntsmen in pink coats reached down for a stirrup-cup brought round by the innkeeper. The ladies rode to hounds, sitting side-saddle, swathed in close-fitting black riding habits with long flowing skirts and called out to each other in high-pitched voices. They turned to wave to friends and gossip while the horses became restless among the waving tails of the hounds, obedient to the word of the Huntsman.

Eliza watched enviously as a girl of her own age in black coat and riding hat tried to control her pony. A groom took its rein.

"There you are now Miss Marianne." he said.

The girl cast a disdainful look at her, but Eliza was already imagining herself galloping across the fields and jumping hedges, her gloved hands guiding her pony into the lead, close behind the huntsmen, everyone shouting "Well done!"

A few weeks later, on the way to school, Eliza was pleased to see the buds fattening on the trees, primroses glowing pale yellow on the banks. Spring was coming. She heard skylarks rising up to sing before dropping down on the heath. Now the land was prepared for sowing by ploughing and rolling - the seed drill pulled by horses. Later on, the swallows came back and the flowers of ox-eye daisies, foxgloves and campions bloomed in profusion along the lane. The beauty of nature surrounding her made her happy in spite of her concern for her future.

In early summer, the reaper machine cut the hay into swathes and the workers turned these with pitchforks to dry before they were gathered up. Eliza played with her friends after school in the hay field until it was cut down and then in the sweet smelling swathes. She looked for birds' nests in the hedgerows and parted the branches carefully to show the little ones. At night, she looked out of the window and saw the moon shining on the wood and glow worms gleaming in the grass.

Father was in a good mood as he had plenty of work. He kissed mother and swung her into a jig round the kitchen while he whooped and jumped as if he was at a party. Eliza laughed - she wished he could always be at home. Now she hated being kept indoors in the school room, writing on her slate and copying proverbs off the blackboard such as "Early to bed and early to rise makes a man healthy wealthy and wise." Although she always liked the art lesson, copying pictures into the blank pages of her exercise book.

On the last day of the summer term, Miss Carter gave the children the day off beforehand to go on the annual school outing to the coast. The yellow and blue painted wagon was decorated with greenery and Eliza and the children climbed aboard. She enjoyed the picnic on the beach, playing on the sand, and paddling in the sea.

In August everyone was needed to harvest the wheat. The weather held and the men set to work. First the edges of the field where the machines couldn't manoeuvre were cut with scythes and Eliza's mother and the other women followed, tying it into sheaves. Eliza minded the baby in the shade of the hedge. Machines cut the rest. Her friend, Jacob rode the offside horse pulling the reaping machine, keeping it close to the standing corn. When it was dry it was carted to the yard and taken inside the big double doors of the old barns.

Eliza went in an empty wagon full of women and children bringing the men's lunch baskets. When they saw the bad tempered old farmer stumping along on his way to inspect the work, they ducked down and threw handfuls of straw and chaff all over him. Eliza was still giggling when, further on, in the harvest field, they jumped out and unloaded the dinners accompanied with bottles and cans of cold tea. As the area of uncut wheat got smaller and smaller, rabbits ran out and the boys with sticks and terrier dogs caught them. The last load of the harvest was decorated with green oak tree branches and Eliza, with her golden hair, blushed with pleasure when she was chosen to represent the ancient corn goddess, Ceres. It was the best day of her life as the foreman put a garland of red poppies and blue cornflowers on her head and hoisted her on top of the wagon to make sure that next year's crop would be a good one. The men went home wearily but shouting for joy in the empty fields.

The farmer invited everyone in to the farmhouse for supper and they sat down in the big kitchen to enjoy roast beef and vegetables followed by plum pudding, washed down with homemade beer. Afterwards Eliza with the women and children were invited into the best parlour while the men stayed to drink and sing the old songs. Eliza was twelve now and relieved that her school days were over. But it was also the end of her childhood and her working life had to begin.

Chapter Two - Into Service

The next day, at breakfast, Eliza's mother said, "Well, my gal, you've finished school now. I've been making enquiries and the rector's wife says there's a place at Grove Farm for a maid - you'll live in there and get some wages too. Just as well, because we need the room, now the younger children are getting bigger."

"But why can't I stay here and help you Mother?" Eliza was devastated, "the older boys still live at home."

"They work on the farm and bring in money - that's why - you can't earn enough, living here. The job pays five pounds a year - you'll be able to send a shilling or two home a month at that rate- you won't need much for yourself – it's all found there."

Eliza knew it was no use arguing with her mother. So, with her hair pinned up for the first time, she walked with her mother over the fields, carrying her little tin box, on her way to earning her own living at a farm a few miles away. It was early morning - the best time of the day, she thought. When they arrived at the old Tudor farmhouse with stone mullioned windows, she paused to take it all in. Early morning mist still hung over the trees and meadows where horses and cows grazed. Apart from the birds singing, it was very quiet in the lane. They walked round the back to find someone to ask. Barns, granaries and sheds were grouped around the farmyard; Eliza felt strange but she was looking forward to starting work.

They knocked at the half-open back door. A maid

came up and took them to see Mrs. Rope, the mistress. Eliza followed her down the passage, although her legs felt weak with fear. A plump, rosy- cheeked woman was sitting at the table in the kitchen, which Eliza thought as big as their whole house. It had window seats, a cool stone- flagged floor and a chimney corner as big as a room.

"Come in, come in. Eliza isn't it? Well, now, how old are you? And what work have you done?"

"She's a good girl, thirteen years old," cut in her mother, "she's helped me in the house with the chores and with the five younger children."

Eliza gave her a reference from the rector's wife, saying she had attended church regularly. The farmer's wife read the letter with a nod, then smiled at her, "Well, you can start off in the kitchen. Your duties are - washing up, preparing the vegetables for meals, and scrubbing down the kitchen, under Cook's guidance. Then clean, polish, make the beds, carry water up for washing in the morning and evening. I will provide print dresses and aprons. Martha will show you your room and what to do." She rose from the table and Eliza kissed her mother goodbye. It was hard to part, now the moment had come, in spite of everything, and it seemed very final. Then Eliza went out of the room with the maid.

The girl showed her the attic where their bedroom was. Eliza followed her up the narrow backstairs and saw a chest of drawers, jug and bowl on a washstand, a hip bath and chamber pots under the beds. She put her things on the empty bed. Then they went downstairs to start work. That night, Eliza lay in bed for a while, feeling strange - she had never been away from her home and her family before. She worried her little sister Maudie, wouldn't settle without her, but she was so tired she soon fell asleep.

Next day they got up early to rake the kitchen fire which was kept in all night and set the table for the servants' breakfast. They had to take hot water from the copper upstairs for the family to wash in, also the shoes and boots which the kitchen boy had cleaned. For breakfast they had porridge. Prayers followed - the girls filed into the parlour which had a green carpet, piano and easy chairs. They knelt in front of the group, with the kitchen boy, the groom and the men of the family behind them. The backhouse boy would tickle them sometimes if he got bored. Eliza twisted away, annoyed. He was a real nuisance, she thought, just trying to get her into trouble. The farmer read from the bible and they sang a hymn, then they were free to get on with their duties.

Later, when Eliza was scrubbing floors, Cook checked her efforts. It was hard, back- breaking work but she was used to that, although she missed being able to go outside in the fresh air. Dinner was at one o'clock, after the family had finished eating. The servants had any food that was left over. Eliza was amazed to see that there was meat every day.

She began to enjoy her time at the farm, because Mrs. Rope was a kind mistress. She looked after Eliza, worked with her and trained her how to do things properly. She even took her into the cool, tiled dairy and showed her how to make cheese and butter. In the evenings, after all the work was done, Eliza sat with the other servants in the inglenook by the fire in the large stone- flagged kitchen and chatted. After a while the mistress would come in and tell the kitchen boy it was bedtime.

The farmer's son, George, was an artist and naturalist and as was his daughter, Hannah. She was making a stained glass window for St. Peter's church in the village. One morning she asked Eliza to step into her workroom so she could do a quick sketch of her. While she drew she commented, "You're a very pretty girl, Eliza, did you know that?"

"No, Miss." Eliza was confused, no-one had ever told her she was good looking before. She didn't know what to say. Hannah went on,

"I used my brother as a model for the men in the East window. Look - Jesus working in the carpenter's shop, St. Peter, a shepherd, a ploughman at work, and a knight in armour -they all look alike, I'm afraid!" She laughed. "I also made the window in the church porch with children singing merrily unto the Lord and playing musical instruments. Making a joyful noise, you know. And I've got an idea for a sculpted panel showing a kneeling angel with a small child or maybe an angel leading a small boy by the hand. I could use your picture for that…"

"O, Miss that would be wonderful. Thank you, Miss, but I must go and get on with my work now", Eliza paused, "I used to like drawing at school …", she laughed awkwardly, "but there's no time for that now."

"Yes, what a shame, I forget - we can't all be ladies of leisure."

One morning, when Eliza went downstairs, there was trouble because nothing had been done and the kitchen was in an uproar. The kitchen boy didn't come in till nine o'clock in the morning. The Mistress was furious.

"Where were you, this morning, Robert? You're supposed be here at six thirty! The maids have had to do your work as well as their own."

Robert stood there, holding his cap and said "Well, Ephraim the groom, he said he wasn't feeling too well last night, so he asked me to stay up and wait for the Master to come home, to look after his horse. Master got back close on midnight, but I got shut out by young Mr. George, when he went outside to feed his dog. He must have thought it was Ephraim in the stable who had his own cottage to go to, so he locked the door. When I had fed and wiped the horse down I found myself locked out so I went down to sleep at my father's house in the village, and it was way past my bedtime, so I overslept this morning. Sorry, Ma'am."

The mistress laughed, "Well, it was an honest mistake so we'll say no more about it." Young George was a bit absent- minded thought Eliza, but he painted lovely pictures and drew sketches of the farm animals and the countryside round about. Old George said he would never make a farmer, so it was just as well he had a weak heart and had to stay at home. Eliza would see him staggering out of the door with his easel and paints "to draw from nature".

Like his sister, George loved children as well as animals and Eliza saw he was never happier than when he was showing village children his collection of guinea pigs and doves. When someone wanted to buy a picture, she noticed, he was always very pleased, even though he had a private income. But he was sensitive and she saw how deeply hurt he was when other artists criticised his work. At times like this, she would bring him a cup of tea and praise his pictures.

On the whole, Eliza liked working for the Rope Family. Working and living away from home, once she got used to it, made her feel grown up and she learned her domestic trade there - the skills and experience she needed; turning out rooms, washing, ironing, watching how Cook made pies and fancy puddings for guests. She earned better money there than she had working in the fields and was proud to send some home to help the family budget.

She had one day off a week and walked home to see the family. When she came home for her summer holiday she brought her Mother a parcel of cast-off clothes the farmer's wife had given her. Mother was delighted, "Oh, I do like something fancy to wear, look at this lovely shawl."

She liked Eliza to wear the best dress and gloves Mrs. Rope had given her for Christmas when she went out in the village, to show off to the neighbours how well she was doing.

On Sundays at the farm, they all went to church. Eliza and Martha sat with Cook on the servants' benches at the back. The Farmer and his family were near the front in their own pew. Eliza loved to hear the stories of Ruth, Esther and Bathsheba which fed her lively imagination. The rector often preached sermons about working hard for your master and she was able to find satisfaction in the dreariest tasks, by doing them well.

One day, after a few years of working at the farm, the rector's wife told her Mother "There is a job going as a maid up at De Vere Hall - your girl should apply for it. It will be a great opportunity to better herself. She can afford the uniform now; dresses, caps and aprons. She's had a few years' experience and will get a good reference from Mrs. Rope. Lord De Vere's a very important man in the neighbourhood, known for having the best of everything. The pay is twenty pounds a year."

Eliza was excited when her mother told her the news. Mother too, was very pleased but gave her a stern warning,

"Don't you be flighty now, my girl - there may be temptations up at the Hall; there are many servants working there indoor and out, including men. Behave yourself."

Eliza said, thinking of old Ephraim the groom and the kitchen boy, "Don't you worry, Mother, I know how to take care of myself."

"Well, you just be careful, that's all I'm saying, my gal - you're starting to fill out now and you'll attract attention, mark my words." It was true, Eliza was no longer a child. She had grown into a beautiful young girl. She was sorry to leave the farm and the Rope family. Mrs. Rope had been like a real mother to her. Eliza kissed her good bye with tears in her eyes.

This time, as Eliza approached her new workplace, she gasped with amazement as the carrier set her down at the gatehouse beside the road; for there, in the distance, framed between huge cedar trees, stood a magnificent redbrick mansion with white stone dressings - a house fit for a king! Indeed she later found out that it was built in the style of the Prince of Wales' house, Sandringham in Norfolk. He was a personal friend of the Baron. The Hall was set in huge gardens with acres of parkland stretching into the distance. Eliza set off down the drive with trembling anticipation to meet her future.

At the back door she was met by a maid and ushered into the Housekeeper's room without delay. A stern middle- aged woman in a black dress looked her up and down as she entered, asked her a lot of questions and then, seemingly satisfied, nodded and said, "Well, I'll take you on, as a lower housemaid - we keep several here as it's such a large establishment. There are eight children in the family as well as his Lordship. There's a lot of work to do - you're not afraid of hard work, I suppose?"

"Oh, no, this is a good chance for me and I mean to do well." said Eliza.

"Very well, then - Keziah will show you your duties as you will be sharing a room with her. You will of course at all times obey the upper servants and do their bidding." Eliza was delighted. She was thrilled to get this place.

She was given a little card with her duties written on it - a strict time table, starting at 6.30am, when she would get up and wake senior staff, until ten o'clock at night. Their room, although small and sparsely furnished with what looked like cast- offs from the rest of the house and plain furniture specially brought in, was a luxury compared to the overcrowded conditions at home. The fire was not lit but she was used to the cold.

Well, her mother needn't worry, Eliza thought as she struggled to smooth down her curly hair into a bun, and tuck it into her cap. She pulled down the black dress she had made herself. It almost covered her feet. A glance in the mirror confirmed that she looked plain and respectable. She noticed over the bed a plaque which read SERVANTS OBEY YOUR MASTERS.

She loved going downstairs into the family rooms to clean before the family came down to breakfast; the first thing she noticed was the perfume of the flowers in the reception rooms; there was a large entrance hall, and leading off it there were ten rooms, including a drawing room, library, and music room. Eliza tended to get lost at first. She gazed in awe at the opulence of the silver candlesticks, paintings, books, carved marble fireplaces, ornate plaster ceilings and marvelled at the spacious light rooms looking out onto the gardens. She felt the soft thick carpet beneath her feet and liked dusting the beautiful furniture. She admired the grand piano, polished all the wood with lavender wax, shaking the cushions and handling the delicate ornaments with care.

Together, she and Keziah laid and lit the fires downstairs, then took hot water upstairs to the family, emptying the chamber pots before a staff breakfast of cold meat with bread and butter and tea. Eliza regretted that the only time she saw the family was at Prayers. After clearing the table, they cleaned the many bedrooms, made the beds, and checked the fires were laid properly. The mistress' bedroom had rose-patterned wallpaper and a pink carpet with great swagged curtains in matching fabric at the windows. Pink silk covered the bed and the chaise-longue in the boudoir. Eliza was enchanted with the beauty of it all and gazed in awe at the crystal cut-glass bottles of perfumes and lotions on the dressing tables, imagining herself sitting there.

In the morning, Eliza wore her print cotton dress. She had morning break at eleven when the Housekeeper issued the orders for the rest of the day. Lunch in the servants' hall at twelve consisted of hot meat and vegetables, followed by pudding or tart. Then she changed into her black dress, carefully adjusting her white lace cap and apron. After she'd helped clear the family lunch, there were some quiet moments in the day when she could read or have a cup of tea, unless the Housekeeper gave her some sewing to do, which she often did.

Once a month the footmen helped lift the heavy furniture in the rooms for them to clean under. The rest of the time Eliza saw them hanging around in the hallway, checking their powdered wigs and uniforms in the mirror, unless they were summoned. At five thirty the servants all had tea of bread and plum cake, after clearing away the family's tea things. In the evening, she turned down the best beds, refilled the jugs with hot water, and closed the curtains. Then they had supper of cold meat, bread and cheese at 9pm before clearing away the family dinner. By ten o'clock Eliza was exhausted and ready for bed.

She liked the camaraderie of the servants' hall, although there was a strict hierarchy below stairs, with junior staff sitting between butler and housekeeper at table. Keziah told her about her own family and the family upstairs.

"Lady De Vere died tragically when the youngest, Master Hugh was only four years old and the eldest daughter, Miss Adeline, eighteen. How much missed she is! Although Nanny, stayed on with them and they have a Governess. Lady De Vere was the daughter of an Earl, you know," Keziah added proudly, basking in the reflected glory of this noble household "and he's descended from French nobility - they had to leave France over their Protestant religion - Huguenots- I think was the name of it. He came into a huge inheritance - it was all over the papers."

Eliza was impressed by these revelations, but carried on with her dusting - the housekeeper was strict and would be sure to check her work.

Life went on quite pleasantly, but sometimes, Eliza felt the monotony of their existence and longed for something a bit more exciting to happen. Then, one day, the three sons came home for the holidays - Masters Percy and Hugh from Eton, and Mr. Frederick from Cambridge University. The household was much livelier when they were at home. They played tricks on the staff and came into the kitchen at all hours asking for cake - upsetting Cook, although Eliza could see she was secretly pleased when Mr. Frederick put his arm round her shoulders and kissed her on the cheek,

"Please, Cook, I'm starving." Suddenly he caught sight of Eliza, and said, "Who's this? A new maid?

Come on and introduce me then."

"Oh, it's only Eliza - she's just started."

Eliza blushed and tried to bustle out of the kitchen quickly with the tray she was carrying, but the young man's enquiring gaze held her and good manners forced her to curtsy and mutter "Mr. Frederick," before she went out red in the face, cursing herself for a fool.

Soon the staff had other things to think about; the Housekeeper assembled them all in the servants' hall one day after breakfast.

"The Prince of Wales is coming to visit the Hall. There will be many guests, selected by the Prince himself, and extra special food such as caviar, truffles and oysters to prepare, to suit His Royal Highness' taste."

Keziah told Eliza that the prince and the Baron had similar tastes in horseracing, shooting and yachting.

"Naturally, the main occupation for the men will be the shooting," the Housekeeper added – Keziah told her the estate had a squad of gamekeepers with blue velvet coats and His Lordship's crest on their brass buttons to ensure that this was excellent. "In the evening there will be cards and dancing," the housekeeper finished.

The whole estate was in an uproar; teams of gardeners raked the gravel, tended the flowerbeds, and mowed the immaculate lawns. Stable lads scurried about, sweeping the yard, brushing the horses to a brilliant shine. Eliza helped open up the guest rooms, make up the fires, air the beds, put on fresh linen sheets and dust the furniture. The stillroom maids were busy bottling fruit and making jams and chutneys. There were fresh flowers everywhere; the Sheraton and Chippendale was polished. Extra staff were brought up from the village to help with the workload. Eliza was exhausted but filled with anticipation and excitement; she felt great pride in helping to make the house and gardens look their best to please the master and his royal visitor.

First to arrive were the visitors' valets and ladies' maids, bringing with them the prospect of meeting old friends and making new ones, exchanging all the latest gossip and catching up with the news. Eliza looked forward to flirting and jollity behind the green baize door in the evenings. All the hard work was compensated by the thought of the generous tips they might get when the party left.

Finally, the cavalcade of carriages that had gone to the station to meet the royal train pulled up noisily outside the front door. Grooms shouted and the horses tossed their heads, harnesses jingling, while valets and footmen hurried out and helped the guests to alight. The housekeeper was waiting to receive them in her best black dress. She curtsied to each one as they swept inside to be met by the butler and host. The butler ushered them into tea in the long hall to meet the rest of the family where a log fire crackled and a warm welcome awaited them after their journey.

In the evenings, the maids watched from upstairs over the banisters, as the elegant guests gathered below. There was to be dancing to an orchestra in the ballroom. Two footmen stood to attention beside the double oak doors. First the ladies went in fluttering their fans with sparkling jewels at their throats, arms and in their hair; then the gentlemen, looking nonchalant and debonair in their high white collars and tailcoats. Eliza saw Frederick looking tall and handsome and suddenly he looked up and she was sure he looked straight at her.

Through the open doorway Eliza could see gilt mirrors reflecting the sparkling chandeliers and the swirling gowns of satin and lace. How she wished she could join the party.

Sighing, she and Keziah went slowly up the stairs to the attics with the music and the laughter singing in their ears. It would be an early start tomorrow, however, and they needed their rest before work began again at six. During the night Eliza was woken by shouts of gentlemen's laughter from downstairs. She wondered if Frederick was among them. In the morning, a valet told them that they had had soda water fights and played practical jokes on each other - a jug of water had fallen onto the head of one of the Prince's friends when he opened his bedroom door and another found pepper in his face towel.

"Oh, that's nothing to the musical beds that's being going on," said another valet, with a wink and a nudge in the girls' direction.

"Hush," hissed Mrs. Marling, "I'll have no such talk at my table, Thank you very much, Arthur - not in front of my girls. Now pass the bacon, if you please, there's plenty of work to do, get on now."

At ten thirty, the gentlemen departed for the shooting, the ladies settled down to chat or write letters in the drawing room. The village boys had been taken out of school to help with the beating and the Prince routed out any shirkers hiding behind their newspapers in a cloud of cigar smoke in the billiard room.

"Come on, old chap - What's that terrible suit you're wearing? - hurry up and change, there's a good fellow."

At lunch time Eliza noticed that the ladies changed into tweeds and followed the men down to the marquee where the food had been set out. Louise, and Annie, the ladies' maids, came down to the servants' hall after getting their ladies ready. They complained "They'll have to pick their way back through the mud and freezing air to the house to amuse themselves before tea. So we'll have to clean their clothes and shoes. Then we have to help them change again - into their lovely tea gowns. Soon it'll be time to help them change for dinner."

Eliza had to run up and downstairs with water for washing and hip baths for both ladies and gentlemen.

It was a relief when Tuesday morning came and the visitors departed, after signing the Visitors' Book. There was some more horseplay when the gentlemen clambered on to the jockeys' chair which had been placed in the hall to check who had put on the most weight during their stay, amid cheers and guffaws of approval. They gave the assembled staff their tips - Eliza was delighted to find she got a guinea - enough to keep her family for a week!

As she turned it over in her hand she thought of the time in the Prince's bedroom when she had bent down to stroke the Irish terrier that came up to greet her when she was putting clean towels out. An old gentleman with a beard had come in unexpectedly and she jumped - she was not allowed to be seen by people upstairs- she must always be invisible while she worked.

"Don't worry, my dear", he said, "I shan't disturb you. I see you like my little dog Jack. You're honoured -he doesn't usually like strangers. You know, your pretty face cheers me up - I'm having a terrible year - Mother is cross with me again - here, see her picture," he said, giving her a guinea.

"Looks like the sort of person who's always cross, to me," said Eliza, without thinking, then, realising that it was the Prince himself, blushed furiously, bobbed her knee, thanked him profusely and fled. His loud laughter followed her down the corridor.

So now life went back to normal and the estate slowly went back about its business; in the morning, she drew the shutters back, and lit the fires. She loved the kitchen, it was a treat for her senses; the butter, milk, cream and cheese were brought in from the dairy. There was a smell of bread baking in the oven. An under-gardener came in early and put fresh flowers in the main rooms of the Hall. One of the other gardeners carried in baskets of vegetables, chicory, endive and fruit - some of it from the hothouses - peaches, melons and grapes. Then mid-morning the butcher delivered meat, and poultry from the home farm. The gamekeeper brought pheasant, duck, partridge, woodcock as well as plenty of hares, and rabbits. She saw that whatever His Lordship wanted was brought to him. There were many people to feed -

twenty in the servants' hall, nine in the family as well as occasional guests. Trades people came to the back door. No one from the village was allowed in the park, let alone the gardens.

The butler ignored her. He was in charge of the male staff - three footmen, valets, and two house boys. It was the housekeeper who was in charge of the nurse, cook, three kitchen maids, two stillroom maids, housemaids, governess, and two ladies' maids. And there were many outdoor staff too, including the Head gardener who had his own cottage, under gardeners, farm bailiff, gasman, coachman, seven grooms and stable hands, dairy maids, carpenter, laundry workers as well as others, like the saddler, wheelwright and blacksmith, who lived in the village and worked for the Hall occasionally.

The upper servants ate with the rest of the staff then retired to the "Pugs' Pantry" as the juniors called it. There Keziah told her, they enjoyed a special desert and coffee in privileged peace. Only then were the junior servants allowed to speak.

"Why are they called Pugs?" asked Eliza.

"Because they have turned down mouths like ladies' pet dogs," returned Keziah giggling. Eliza noticed that some of the other servants spoke with strange accents and mentioned it to Keziah when they were alone together.

"They come from Scotland, Yorkshire, London and other Shires, that's why. The lady's maid and the governess come from foreign parts - Louise is from Paris, France and Fraulein Shwarz from Germany. They answered advertisements in the newspapers and came by train."

Eliza was impressed. She had never met anyone who wasn't from her own village before. Keziah went on,

"One of the reasons why the master is such a big name in the district - apart from the fact that he's an aristocrat, a wealthy baron with twenty thousand acres, including five farms, is that he breeds Suffolk Punches and owns successful racehorses. He keeps three men just to see after the stallions. There are scores of horses but the greatest of them is Big Boy. He's won so many brass medals at the County Shows he can't carry them all on his harness. Men came from all over to see the horses but they hardly ever see Big Boy. He's hid up and not to be looked at."

"How do you know so much about it, Keziah?"

"My father's a horseman. He used to work here. They love the horses like friends. The ploughmen talk softly to their teams all day long and you see the horse's ears turn back, listening. Sometimes the men sing to them in the fields. They have secret medicines which they whisper about in the tack room, but they stop talking quick if anyone comes in."

"I wonder if I'll get a chance to go down to the stables to see the horses, Keziah? I do miss working on the farm near my village."

"Well, don't let anyone catch you at it is all I say," replied Keziah.

"What's Lord De Vere like?" asked Eliza, changing the subject.

"He's the gentleman with the black beard and lorgnette. Everyone's scared of him. He's always immaculate of course, Arthur sees to that. Mainly he's a farmer and landowner, but he also has East India company shares, interests in banking and the West Indies sugar trade. He succeeded his father as baron when he was very young. Now he's Justice of the Peace, Deputy Lieutenant of the county and honorary Colonel of the Suffolk Artillery, the Militia. Also he's a Steward of the Jockey Club that controls British Horse racing and last, but not least, Conservative Member of Parliament." Keziah ended triumphantly.

Eliza felt a chill going through her at all this, and fervently hoped that she never made him angry. Before prayers at eight thirty in the morning, she saw him going over the accounts with the estate manager in his office, while the grooms were preparing the coach and horses to take him later on to the Magistrates Court.

On the other hand, it seemed to Eliza that the daughters of the house were only expected to look decorative.

"Tell me about the daughters," she said.

"Adeline, the eldest, is the Mistress." Keziah told her "She had to take over the duties of hostess and household manager for her father, when her mother died ten years ago. Marianne's the youngest. She's only sixteen. She's still kept in the schoolroom with her governess. Miriam, Cecilia, and Ruby are all out in society. They've been presented at court. As daughters of a peer, they got a kiss on the cheek from Queen Victoria, not just a handshake like the others. They always go up to London for The Season - April to August. Annie, the lady's maid, goes everywhere with them – so that they don't meet the 'wrong' type of person. She tells us all about it."

"What does Marianne do all day up there?" asked Eliza.

"Well, Herbert, the footman waits on them. He says the schoolroom is quite plainly furnished. The governess teaches her drawing, music, and they read books and poetry. The boys went away to boarding school when they were seven, but the girls just learn things they need to make them good wives in the marriage market; manage a home, sit on committees and do charity visiting. That's what the London Season is, so they can make a `good match."

Eliza asked "What do they do the rest of the year then?"

"Mainly reading books from the Library, doing embroidery, playing the piano, riding and hunting. Annie complains when they ride out hunting - their riding habits get filthy dirty and soaking wet. Of course they socialize too and have long mealtimes, as you know."

Eliza only saw them when they attended morning prayers, conducted by the Baron, or went to church on Sunday with the family. Marianne came down after nursery tea to the drawing room to sit with the adults for an hour.

On their frequent visits to the kitchen, the younger boys made a favourite of Eliza and gave her some of their sweets. She could handle them alright and grew fond of them, they were so appreciative for everything the servants did for them. Mr. Frederick was different. She found his awakening interest in her disturbing and hoped he would soon have to go back to Cambridge;

he kept brushing his hand against hers and started asking her to go for a walk with him. One day, she had to go to the village on an errand for the housekeeper, and he seized his chance to join her along the path. She started to run but he chased her until she was out of breath. When he came up to her, her bonnet was loose and her hair fell round her face in golden curls. "What pretty hair, you have Eliza," he said, touching it gently.

"I mustn't be seen with you like this Mr. Frederick - it's not right - I'll be told off."

"Nobody's going to know - and surely, it's Freddie, now - we're friends aren't we?"

"Yes. Well. No - we can't be, can we? - I'm a servant and you're my master's son." With that, she hurried away, taking the short cut to the village.

Chapter Three - The Hon. Frederick

There was chaos in the kitchen next day, when Eliza had finished her chores and she was hoping to relax in the maids' sitting room after lunch. She was reading a novel called `The Duke and the Parlourmaid` at the moment and couldn't wait to get back to it. However, fate intervened in the shape of the flustered cook who called out to her,

"Take this tray up to Nanny, Eliza. Everyone else is too busy."

"Er, Nanny? - which is her room?"

"On the top floor at the back, next to the Day Nursery," replied Cook, getting impatient.

Eliza climbed up the many stairs slowly. Her feet were hurting and she didn't want to go. Searching along the corridor she passed a large, light room with a rocking horse, bookshelves, toy soldiers, building blocks, and dolls' house. This must be the Day Nursery, she thought. She tapped on the door next to it.

"Come in," called out a gentle voice.

Eliza entered a pleasant room furnished with bed, chair and dressing table. The walls were pink. The bedcover and curtains were in a matching flower pattern.

"Thank-you, dear," said the old lady resting in her armchair. "You're new, aren't you?"

"Yes," said Eliza, they sent me because everyone's so busy downstairs now the boys are home for the holidays."

"Ah, the boys…" Nanny settled back in her chair.

"They always come up to see their old Nanny as soon as they arrive, you know. Of course, I remember when they were born. Sit down dear."

Eliza did so, feeling that she was in for a long chat. The poor old soul seemed lonely, shut away up here away from the other servants, so she didn't mind too much. Nanny was getting into her stride now,

"When Frederick was born, after three girls, there was much rejoicing. The celebrations we had! There was an ox roast in the park for all the tenants and villagers and fireworks in the evening. A party for the local dignitaries and for the servants. Of course I was given sole charge of the precious child from the start and told to watch over him night and day."

Goodness, thought Eliza, he was treated like royalty. I was the first daughter after six boys, but I think Mother was just glad she had someone to help with the housework and childcare at last!

"The christening was a great occasion," went on Nanny, pouring herself a cup of tea, "How he cried as the rector poured holy water over his head and named him Frederick Archibald Charles. All the local gentry were there to welcome the baron's first son, heir to the title and estate. The Baroness looked pleased and proud - she had done her duty at last. Later on she had two more sons. There were two more girls too, but the nursery maids looked after them," Nanny added as an afterthought.

"See what the estate carpenter has made for you, Master Frederick!" I remember saying to him. "Now, Miriam, Adeline, Cecelia, make way for your little brother, let him have first choice of the toys -he will be

Lord De Vere one day and take your father's place at the head of the family."

"But he's only three," they complained, "we're older than him."

"Hush, girls," I told them. "He's a boy. The title and estate must pass to a male heir. You girls will marry one day and be mistresses of your own households."

Eliza thought back to her family and remembered her brothers were always treated like little lords by her mother.

At lunch time, I was strict about manners. I said, "Sit up straight, children, don't put your elbows on the table. We always said grace together, as is proper,

Thank you Lord as we sit here
With feast and fire and naught to fear;
Pity the unhappy poor -
And bless this house for evermore. Amen."

How those girls complained as I uncovered the dishes the nursery maid had brought "Not boiled mutton and milk pudding again!"

Fussy lot, thought Eliza – we'd have killed for that food.

"Plain food is best for young stomachs," I told them, "now eat up or no cake at teatime."

Eliza stirred restlessly in her chair, but Nanny was enjoying her reminiscences, she seemed to have forgotten she was there.

"After lunch and a nap, they got out their stamp collections and scrap books until it was time for a walk. After tea I helped them dress in their best clothes and brushed their hair, ready to take them down to see

Mama and Papa in the drawing room. Sometimes they put on little plays and concerts for the servants and the guests, who said

"What delightful children you have, Lord De Vere."

"Well, of course, I took it as a personal compliment. But I think the children were relieved to get away from the formality of the grown- ups, and climb back upstairs to the night nursery to get ready for bed. They knelt down to say their prayers, then I read them a story before they went to sleep. I loved them as I would my own and they loved and respected me. The nursery was their world."

Now Nanny nodded off to sleep in her chair and Eliza crept out of the room with the tray, so as not to disturb her, thankful to get away at last, even though she had found the old lady's stories about Freddie's childhood very interesting.

As she climbed back downstairs, she thought about his strict childhood and how little he had seen of his parents. He'd been sent away to boarding school when he was only seven. She felt a bit sorry for him and decided to be friendlier to him when he next spoke to her.

So the next day, when Freddie came into the kitchen after luncheon, and gave her a note asking her to meet him at the stables that afternoon, she walked down there. She wanted to see the horses and this was a golden opportunity. As she approached, he came out of one of the loose boxes and pulled her inside.

"Come in here, then we won't be seen by the grooms. Nanny said you'd been to see her yesterday."

"Yes, I took her tray up and she told me all about you and your sisters growing up here in the Nursery."

"She was devoted to us, especially me of course."

"Sounds like you were thoroughly spoilt!"

Freddie laughed. "Cheeky girl, you must pay for that later! You see, we spent most of our time with the servants. We always got on well. They were on our side against the adults – ignoring the rules, letting us off punishments. Cook let us roll out dough and make biscuits. The lady's maid showed the girls how to knit, and crochet. We weren't allowed to play with the village children. How I hated Sundays," Frederick went on "Normal activities were forbidden and everyone had to attend church. True, the De Vere family pew at the front was the only place to have any heat. If the sermon bored him, father poked the stove fire so loudly that the preacher had to finish quickly."

"He still does," giggled Eliza.

"Yes, of course, you know." Freddie answered, smiling down at her. "In the afternoon, we were only allowed to play with the wooden Noah's ark or read religious books. Even Mama daren't knit, sew or play cards on Sundays for fear of shocking the staff - she had to keep up appearances in front of the servants who were often in the room".

How strange, Eliza thought, to be constantly surveyed by other people even when you are at home, relaxing.

"When I was seven," he went on, "my country paradise ended and I was sent away to prep school. At thirteen, I went on to Eton, my father's old school. We learned to be stoic and self- disciplined."

"What does stoic mean?" asked Eliza.

"Enduring and tough, without complaining" he answered. "Conditions were fairly basic. There was fagging as well - that's when younger boys have to wait on older ones. Sometimes you got beaten if you were late or forgot something."

"How terrible!" exclaimed Eliza. Frederick shrugged and went on

"Nanny noticed the bruises when I got home,

`Oh, Master Frederick, let me see - you're hurt` she said.

"Don't fuss, Nanny," I told her

"Father says I need to get away from your apron strings if I'm to grow up to be a man -but thank-you for sending the jam and fruit cake."

Nanny just sniffed. "It's good to know I still have my uses."

"So did you enjoy school at all?" asked Eliza.

"Of course. I studied Classics and Literature. Luckily, I'm good at football and cricket. I made lots of friends.

"Weren't your sisters jealous of you boys?"

"Oh, no, the girls looked up to us. When we came home from boarding school, we were lordly and mysterious, having experienced a new world. They have to stay at home until they get married."

Eliza suddenly realized that she must get back to her duties, it was getting late in the afternoon. "Thank you for letting me see the horses, I must go back now."

"Not before you pay the fine for being rude to me." Freddie grabbed her and kissed her before she could push him away and hurry off to the servants' hall.

There, a footman was reading out some scandal from the newspaper.

"Elizabeth Acford has brought a case claiming Lord Huntingtower seduced her while she was in service to him. He took her through a "mock marriage" in front of another servant, had three children by her, but then deserted her."

Maybe this should have sounded warning bells in Eliza's ears but the butler came in at this point and told him

"Put that away, Albert - while I'm in charge of this house, you'll show some respect for your betters and know your place. Let them as are natural leaders, rule and such as you, defer to them."

During staff tea, Eliza asked the butler to tell her more about the family history. He was gratified that she showed an interest in her employers and took it as a chance to show off his knowledge.

"Well, the family were expelled from their noble estate in France after the Massacre of St. Bartholomew in 1572 when the Huguenots (French Protestants) were killed by the Catholics. They fled to Switzerland where they prospered."

His youngest son came to England and accumulated an immense fortune in banking and the sugar trade in London; he owned sugar plantations in Jamaica. He bought country estates for his sons, was made a baron and left large fortunes to each of them in his will."

"Thank you," said Eliza, looking round at the other staff who were stifling yawns and glaring at her because they'd heard it all before,

"That's amazing."

She could imagine Frederick as he stirred next day when his valet came into the room, opened the curtains and said "Good morning, Sir". He would put the tea tray by the bed, prepare his bath and help him shave and dress; every item cleaned and repaired ready for this and every occasion. And Frederick saying nonchalantly,

"Those shirts are no good to me, now, Cooper - sell or keep them as you wish."

Eliza brought up the hot water and knew Cooper helped him change during the day and stayed up to get him ready for bed at night, however late the hour.

At the same time she knew Adeline, Miriam, Cecilia, Ruby and Marianne were being woken by their ladies' maids with their tea on a tray. They laid out their clothes for the day, prepared their baths and helped them with their toilette as many garments fastened at the back; they made, repaired and laundered their clothes, including their fine silk and lace things. They applied beauty treatments and dressed their hair fashionably. Louise was French, from Paris - and liked her mistresses to spend a lot of time and money on their clothes and go out a great deal. She could be temperamental and flighty at times, but was full of style and sparkling vivacity.

When they were in the country, Eliza saw that the girls spent their time riding and hunting. They also played tennis, croquet and practiced archery outside on the sweeping lawns of the house. Sometimes guests came so they got to know the right sort of people.

On another occasion, Freddie told her:

"I was only twelve when my mother died, perhaps

that's why I'm attracted to a warm, kind- hearted girl like you, Eliza. She was always a bit remote anyway but she lit up the nursery when she visited us - wise and powerful, busy with things we didn't understand. My eldest sister, Adeline, was only eighteen at the time. She had to take over mother's duties and act as father's household manager, with the housekeeper and butler's help, of course." He laughed as he recalled, "Cook curbed her wilder suggestions and managed to get the menu exactly as she had planned it herself, while making her feel important at the same time."

Normally, Eliza only saw members of the family at morning prayers, church on Sunday or at servants' dances. She watched the ladies come rustling in, on a cloud of perfume and sink languidly down into their chairs. They were so graceful, she loved watching them and admired the way they knelt for prayers, slanting forward with the sole of one dainty shoe in front of another. They were tall and slender and Eliza thought them very aristocratic- looking. They took no notice of her at all. But their younger brothers had a crush on her and kept furtively glancing at her. Frederick always passed close to her chair and brushed against her.

The family called her by her first name. The younger boys were openly friendly but the daughters were more reserved. They went out in the pony carriage to visit the elderly and sick to take gifts of food, clothing or medicine. They made and gave out Christmas presents, and put on an annual play or treat for the village children. They knew everyone and took great interest in their welfare. The boys ran a sports club, and the girls taught Sunday school and trained the village choir. Nanny always taught them that `From those to whom much is given, much is expected.`

The Baron was all powerful, his opinions faultless - he was the great authority. Always busy, he personally controlled the Militia, the Bench, the schools, the church, farm leases and many jobs. He conducted family prayers when he was at home. If he was autocratic and arrogant, this was considered just another privilege of rank. Eliza saw that he loved his children, guided their upbringing, enjoyed their lively games, gave them generous presents, treats and outings. Nevertheless, he could enforce absolute obedience and insisted on good behaviour.

Eliza felt her heart lurch whenever she saw Frederick. He was twenty one, two years older than she was. He was handsome, dark haired and tall and she was aware of his presence, living, as she did, close to the family, coming into the family rooms for prayers and to clean and service them. Eliza was innocent and like other girls in the village, knew nothing about sex. He seemed like a god to her, who had seen little of the world and grown up in poverty.

One day he met her in the lane and swept off his hat in a low bow that made her feel like a princess.

"Eliza come for a walk with me, I'm lonely and bored and need someone to talk to."

His voice was quiet and natural and he was pleasant and well-mannered to her. She had always refused before, but she was flattered by his interest in her, a lowly servant, doing dirty jobs, cleaning and emptying slop buckets. She was normally not allowed to talk or look at the people upstairs unless they spoke to her first. Forced to turn away or flatten herself against the wall if one of them passed her in the passage, it seemed to her like a dream come true that someone like him could care for her, pay her compliments, and want her company. Frederick told her, as they walked through the fields,

"Did Nanny tell you how, after lessons in the morning, we visited the home farm; fed the animals, collected eggs, and helped with milking? Then we went into the cool, sweet- smelling, tiled dairy and tried out the butter churn. In summer we went hay making. We played in the garden, under the trees with her looking on. We ran on smooth green lawns down shady avenues, past ornamental flower beds, statues and fountains. It was a private safe world; an enchanting playground; with space for cricket, croquet and made up games. Trees to climb, a lake and pond for swimming, boating and skating; slopes for tobogganing down when the snow was thick on the ground in winter."

"An outdoor life is healthy and natural," Nanny always said. "My brothers and I jumped the brook, climbed into the huge oak trees, flew kites, and fired pea shooters and water pistols at each other or the gardeners."

"Sounds wonderful" said Eliza, thinking what a nuisance they must have been and remembering her own childhood chores and hard work.

He went on "If it was too cold to play outside, we ran down the corridors and played battledore and shuttlecock in the hall. There were lots of pets too - indoors and out- canaries, cats, dogs, and rabbits. We loved the horses and ponies best. On our ponies, usually with a groom, or on drives and walks with the governess, we explored the estate and surrounding countryside, learning about nature and country life. When we were older, we rode off on our own in the park among the huge trees, and explored the wild, untamed woods. Everyone we met knew us and smiled respectfully; touched their caps or curtsied to us."

"Didn't you have any friends of your own age then?" asked Eliza, remembering her own communal village life.

"Not really, but sometimes, parties were arranged in the country as well as in London," replied Frederick. "We went to the seaside in late summer. But the gardeners and grooms were our best friends and teachers. The girls loved Cook best. The footman did card tricks, told us riddles and gave us ginger beer or lemonade. The housemaids were always glad to see us and applauded when we dressed up and acted plays. We were taught riding, driving and hunting by the groom and coachman. It was exciting to jump hedges and ditches and be "blooded" at our first kill. The gamekeeper showed us how he reared game birds and taught us how to shoot and fish."

Eliza was fascinated but had to go. "Look, I must hurry back", she said, seeing the house appear through the trees, "Goodbye, Frederick."

Arriving in the kitchen, Eliza read out the new notice that the housekeeper had just pinned up. "Servants are not allowed to mix with members of the opposite sex or have followers; sober clothes to be worn off duty."

"They don't want us going courting in case we get wed and they have the trouble of getting new staff," said Keziah standing beside her. "I can't afford to marry young anyway - my parents need the money I send, and I need to save up to get married. I reckon I'll leave service in my late twenties." Eliza nodded. Keziah was always so sensible, she already had her life mapped out.

"But we do have dances. Just as well, it's so dull here, stuck away in the country with no neighbours or village life. When the family have birthdays, coming of age or weddings, things like that, they have celebrations for us to join in. The balls cheer you up, and give you something to look forward to. At Christmas - there'll be special food, drink and entertainment for the servants. In summer we have a day out, a picnic or trip to the seaside."

Eliza wondered if she would see Frederick at these events.

"I can't get over how much good food we get here!" she said at lunchtime.

"It's to keep our strength up for a sixteen hour working day" said Albert. "Most of it's produced on the home farm." Apart from three good meals a day, bread and cheese mid- morning, tea, cocoa or beer and afternoon tea with bread and butter and sometimes, cake, at four, filled out Eliza's slight figure and greatly improved her health.

She accepted the rules and standards imposed on her; the strict dress code both at work and in free time.

The housekeeper gave the maids a lecture,

"Fashionable items such as fringes, ribbons or artificial flowers and jewellery are strictly forbidden. You must wear plain dark dresses and bonnets even on your days off. The master and mistress take a personal interest in you. They're concerned for your welfare. That's why they have drawn up these codes of conduct for you - to protect you. In return you're expected to be humble, respectful and in uniform. It's a privilege for you to work for such wealthy, influential people."

Lord De Vere had provided billiards, chess and draughts for the male staff; the menservants played the concertina and female staff read books and magazines. Eliza was now reading a romantic novel called "Kitty and the Count," in which the heroine was a servant girl who fell in love with a Lord and married him. Others knitted, sewed or socialised with staff from nearby houses in the evenings or at tea in the afternoons. They sat in the servants' hall on benches at a large table, overlooking the kitchen courtyard. Free time was usually an afternoon off per week or every other Sunday and a fortnight's holiday a year.

Eliza made friends and grew in confidence. She wrote and read letters from home and kept in touch with family and friends. She got to know those who worked at the house and on the estate. As time went by she felt accepted, she belonged. She was excited at seeing so much of life among a number of strange men and women. Sometimes tensions and arguments flared up but there was also friendship, romance and marriage. In spite of the silence rule at meals, there was often a bit of footsy going on under the table as the tall, handsome footmen flirted with the maids causing blushes and stifled giggles.

Eliza didn't take them seriously. She and the other maids all went into one room at night and had a good chat. The footmen gossiped, joked and played pranks on each other. Indoor and outdoor staff, isolated in the country, made friends and helped each other. They shared news and job possibilities with visiting staff, including stories about who was good to work for and who wasn't.

Sleeping quarters, even staircases were separate - the maids' corridor was called `The Virgins' Wing`. All maids had to be in their room by ten and the housekeeper kept a close eye on them.

When Eliza went home for a visit, her mother said, "Why Eliza you're almost a stranger."

"Well, it's because my life at the Hall is so different to home, Mother."

"I suppose you're part of the big house family now."

"Yes, I feel I belong there."

It was true - She felt a shared enjoyment and pride in the wealth, beauty and belongings of the house and estate. A strong bond of love and loyalty for the family.

She identified with them; adopting their attitudes and habits. Living in the stately home atmosphere, among their ways of thinking, living and feeling, she became like them. Eliza found it impossible to live among such beauty without it getting under her skin; she learnt taste and appreciation - to distinguish what is good and what is not; she dusted the books lining the shelves and eventually began to read them; overheard conversations made her want to know more. She learnt moral values, not always by example but by observation and comparison. She absorbed all these things. This was her real education.

She wasn't really listening when her mother said "You must soon save up for your bottom drawer - for the things you'll need when you marry." She was thinking about Freddie.

She had changed; had learned so much, become more articulate and experienced in upper class ways. Her job as an indoor servant gave her better working conditions and status than many other workers in the village. She found the old village women's talk coarse and countrified now. Her parents were proud of her supple figure, clear eyes, strong white teeth, and fresh colour, and amazed by the stories of the luxury and high life she had seen. Not to mention the modern facilities of gas lighting, indoor taps and water closets. She crooked her little finger and sipped her tea delicately, discussing the latest fashion or serial novelette.

On Christmas Eve, the village bell ringers took their hand bells all around the parish. They tramped through the snow and were invited into farms and big houses to ring the bells to entertain the occupants, in the big porch or the drawing room. They were late coming that year and the Mistress of De Vere Hall, realising the maids would not settle down until they came, although it was past their usual bedtime, let them stay up late. That night the bells were rung in the porch and Eliza enjoyed serving the musicians coffee with a strong dash of rum. The shepherd was with the ringers and when they rang the bells outside he rested his lantern on his crook. Even though they had drunk beer, gin, wine and rum at every stop, the leader insisted they play all the set tunes amidst the jollifications even after a twelve mile walk and much the worse for wear.

There was a huge tree at the Hall. Eliza helped decorate it with spun glass ornaments. She and the other servants put up great swags of holly, ivy and mistletoe on the grand staircase and mantelpieces. On Christmas morning, after church, she lined up with the others to receive their presents from Lord De Vere. But she was disappointed to get a length of material, as the all the maids did, to make a plain servant's dress.

However, she looked forward excitedly to the evening; there were carol singers from the village, then they went back to the warmth of the servants' hall, where a great feast was piled on the refectory tables - roast turkey, game pie, plum pudding, and beer in big jugs. Then the fiddlers arrived, French chalk was sprinkled around the floor and the servants' ball began.

As was traditional, the Master opened it in the arms of the housekeeper and Miss Adeline followed, partnered by the butler. The footmen asked the young ladies of the house to dance. As they were not used to dancing, they trod on their feet a lot. Frederick and his younger brothers took the opportunity to dance with the maids. He took Eliza's hand and slipped his arm around her waist. They gazed into each other's eyes as the strains of a Viennese waltz carried them round the room in a dream.

"You're the loveliest girl in the county, Liza," he breathed into her ear. Her heart was pounding so much she couldn't speak. After a time the family withdrew and left the staff to enjoy themselves, which was a relief to everyone except Eliza.

She had to help with the annual dole of shirts, petticoats, sheets and coal to the poor of the parish and a Christmas party for the school children with a huge tea in the dining room; a white cloth was laid out with sandwiches, cakes, pastries and jellies. Then all the men who worked on the estate waited in the yard and came cap in hand to where the baron, his family and the Land Agent stood at the end of a long trestle table and were given one or two ducks according to their family size. They wished the workers "Happy Christmas" and the men stumped off into the night.

Eliza was turning down the beds upstairs. She was surprised when the young master himself came in. "What are you doing here, Freddie?" she gasped in dismay.

"Don't worry - no-one can hear us up here. I've got a present for you - look."

"Oh, Freddie, a ring - I've never had anything so lovely. Does this mean…?"

"Yes - I love you. Aren't you going to give me a kiss to thank me?"

She was unsure. She felt vulnerable, alone.

"You're such an innocent, Eliza. Come here - I thought you were supposed to be obedient to your lord and master. "He kissed her gently, then more passionately.

"You don't know how I've longed for you. I can't

sleep. I can't eat. Just let me touch you." All the pent up desire they felt for each other poured out as he pulled her down onto the bed. He caressed her and they made love.

Afterwards he said "My darling, now off you go - I've got to change for dinner. Oh, better keep quiet about this for now."

She was upset at first, losing her virginity but went downstairs in a dream, hiding the ring in her pocket. He loved her. He had chosen her above his own circle. She would marry him and be a lady like the heroine in the book she was reading. She would be the mistress, wear fine clothes and have no work to do.

Despite being caught several times on the back stairs by the housekeeper, Frederick continued to pursue her. He got to know her whereabouts and turned up any time he could catch her alone. He was loving and sweet and she adored him and wanted to show her love for him.

All too soon he had to go back to university and the younger boys back to school. Life was flat for Eliza and she didn't see the family much now. She was reminded afresh that she was one of the under servants. The family consulted senior staff like the Cook, Head Gardener, Head Gamekeeper, Stud Manager but they rarely even acknowledged the maids - their work had to be done when family members were out of their rooms. Sometimes his Lordship would smile and say in passing

"Hot weather for scrubbing."

Or Miss Adeline would ask kindly "How are you getting on, Eliza?"

She felt uncomfortable when the Housekeeper took the maids into her room one day to give them a lecture;

"Be careful to preserve your virtue, girls. If you get into the family way it will mean instant dismissal without a reference. I remind you the fate of unwed mothers is grim." She glared round at the assembled girls. Eliza felt herself blushing. She felt guilty. Surely the Housekeeper didn't know about her and Frederick - it didn't show, did it, that she wasn't a virgin anymore? Afterwards the head housemaid said darkly,

"At my last place they'd be funny things going on and when there was trouble, it would be the workhouse. Some went in to have the baby and that was where they'd finish."

Eliza just lived for the university vacations at Easter and summer when Freddie returned home and they resumed their affair. She had never been happier and the days flew by. Enlivened by the thought of seeing him again, she had a special glow, a secret smile.

Keziah noticed and said "You're in a funny mood these days, Eliza. Try and keep your mind on your work, will you. You're not doing your fair share. I can't keep clearing up after you. I shall complain to the Housekeeper."

"Please don't, Keziah….it's just that I feel so tired these days." Once she even fainted in the privy. "What's the matter with me? She wondered. As the weeks went by, she had to lace herself in tighter to hide her swelling stomach. It wasn't just the extra food, she thought, and began to be increasingly anxious about what to do.

One hot summer's day, Freddie led her down to the summer house, which was almost hidden by a canopy of white, heavily scented roses. He pulled back the curtain of soft fragrant blooms, pushed open the door. She hesitated, looking around her nervously. Servants weren't allowed in the garden.

"No one will see us here," he whispered and she followed him inside.

He spread out the blanket he had brought on the stone floor and kissed her tenderly. She was overcome with weakness and the heady perfume. The garden was full of birdsong. His lips tasted of red wine. She responded to his caresses.

"Oh, Eliza, you're so lovely, I … love you." She put her arms around him and shuddered with pleasure.

Afterwards, she gazed at him as he collapsed beside her, smiling triumphantly. He idly stroked her belly.

"Putting on weight are we?" he teased.

"No, Freddie…. I'm pregnant."

"Oh Lord. Look, keep quiet about it and I promise I'll look after you. I'll think of something."

But by the end of summer the truth came out. The Housekeeper called her into her room. Her eyes looked her up and down searchingly. "Sit down, Eliza. What's this I hear about you slacking in your work?"

"I haven't been feeling well, Miss."

"Tell me the truth. Is there something you're not telling me? Have you had your monthlies lately?"

"Well…"

"I suspected as much - You're having a baby. Disgraceful! You'll have to go, Eliza. And it's a pity. You could have worked your way up here as I did. Go upstairs and pack your things at once. Who's the father - is it one of the male staff?"

"It was Freddie, he said he loved me!"

"We have no Freddie working here. You don't mean - Mr. Frederick…. ". She frowned. "Don't speak of this to anyone. I will inform the mistress." Eliza left the room. Mrs. Harris bustled upstairs and knocked on the Mistress' door.

"It's one of the maids, Ma'am, Eliza. I've had to dismiss her for immoral conduct, but she says Mr. Frederick is involved."

"I see…leave the matter with me - I will find out the truth. And tell no-one. I don't want any idle talk, you understand. This must go no further."

Eliza hurried away in tears to find Freddie. She knew he would be in the library at this time of day.

"Frederick, the housekeeper's found out about the baby and dismissed me, I have to go at once."

"Don't worry my love, I'll come with you - we'll run away together. Meet me in my room. I'll pack some things and we'll catch the train to London."

Eliza hurriedly put her few belongings into her tin trunk and ran downstairs to Freddie's room. But when she knocked on the door, it was flung open by the Mistress.

"So it is true. You've deceived me by sneaking around behind my back! This ends now, do you hear me? Eliza, go at once and never try to contact Frederick again. For his sake don't try to drag him down to your level."

Eliza felt guilty and ashamed as she went downstairs. By now the whole household could hear the Baron shouting at Freddie in his study.

She fled the Hall with their insults ringing in her ears.

Chapter Four - The Workhouse

Eliza walked home to the little cottage in Pump Square. She didn't know if her parents would have her at home. When she pushed open the door of the cottage, she could see into the kitchen and overhear the voices of her younger sisters. Her mother was sweeping down the stairs, but at the sound of footsteps, she looked over the banisters and said

"Why, Eliza, it's not your day off is it?"

"I was sent home, Mother."

Her mother came downstairs and peered at her.

"You do look poorly, I must say. What's happened? Are you ill?"

"I've been dismissed, Mother!" Eliza started to cry and threw herself against her mother's ample bosom.

"There now, it's no use crying, what's done is done. What a shame! We thought you were doing so well, sending us money and all. Tell me what happened."

Eliza paused. The girls had stopped talking and the front door was still open. She said

"Shall we go into the parlour? We can talk quietly there."

Eliza closed the front door and they went into the parlour. They sat opposite each other by the window, anxiety etched on both their faces.

"I had to leave, mother. I'm going to have a baby."

"Oh, Eliza. No. What's to be done? You come home without a job and in disgrace - our eldest daughter, what an example is this for your sisters? No reference and in your condition, you won't be able to find work. And the whole village will soon be alive with gossip!"

Her mother thought quickly, "We must keep the whole thing secret. Otherwise it'll be public shame and humiliation that'll reflect on everyone in the family, not just you and the child. Who is the father? I think we're entitled to know that."

"It's the master's son, mother. He told me he loved me."

"Well he won't marry you. Gentry and servants don't mix. You should have kept yourself pure. It was up to you to stop things getting out of hand. He may deny everything - you can't prove it was him. A young man like that - he's bound to want to sow his wild oats. Well, at least the child should get some support, but that still doesn't answer the question of who's going to look after it? Your father's fifty eight and I'm fifty three with four children still at home; and there's my father, eighty-eight. I thought my child bearing days were over."

The cottage was crowded; John, eighteen, a merchant seaman, was home on leave, Arthur, a general labourer of sixteen, Thomas, fourteen, unemployed, Maud, a pupil teacher of twelve and Rose, aged ten, nearly finished her schooling. When Father came in and heard what had happened, he was angry. But his face was grave with concern as he held her close -

"Nay girl; never speak of this again. The secret must die with you - for all our sakes. You'll have a husband and children of your own one day. You're still young - you can start a new life. It's a disgrace, the gentry should protect our pure young women from these predatory men. I've a good mind to go up there to see his Lordship and sort this out. Why should we be left with all the responsibility and expense? After all we are respectable, God-fearing folk!"

Mother said "One thing's clear - you must go to the Workhouse in Wickham Market and stay there until the baby's born. There's no room for you here. And then, I suppose I'll have to care for it. After all it is our own family, but you'll have to go away when it's weaned. Somewhere where nobody knows you and start a new life."

The news that Eliza was home spread and the gossips speculated on the reason. Soon everyone in the village looked at Eliza with pity or superiority. Eliza was relieved that her mother was going to take her child when it was born. She knew children who had to stay in the workhouse had a loveless, deprived existence. For that reason very few babies were born out of wedlock.

It wasn't long before their neighbour knocked at the cottage door and came in, eager for the details. She had guessed that Eliza was in trouble and heard tongues wagging around the village.

"You poor dear," she said to Eliza, "Never you mind what folks say about you, it's only the good girls like you that have babies; the others is too artful!"

This made the poor girl burst into tears again. The neighbour put an arm around her shoulders and patted her back soothingly. "There, there, such a clean, quiet girl as you an all - it isn't fair, that you be taken advantage of like this." she was secretly pleased that it hadn't happened to her own daughter- that Mrs. Stone needed to be taken down a peg or two, she thought, and Eliza had been getting too full of herself lately. Pride goes before a fall, they say. She went on

"Tis a moment of weakness only, not a sin. I'm sure you've learned your lesson."

Like other desperate people who had fallen to the bottom of society - the homeless, the poor, the insane, the aged, orphans - Eliza had nowhere else to go but the workhouse. She would be put to work to pay off her debt to the parish for her keep. She knew these bleak institutions were built to dissuade paupers applying for `poor relief`. The conditions were harsh to punish the inmates, to provide physical and moral rehabilitation for unmarried mothers, and prostitutes. There, they worked at cleaning and laundry, received religious instruction and learned the skills required to lead an honest, respectable life.

She decided to go for a walk by the sea to escape her gloomy thoughts. She struggled along the shingle on the endless, empty beach, looking for help in the vast expanse of sea and sky. Nothing but greyness everywhere. She passed a Martello tower built to protect England from Napoleon's invasion. It loomed up desolate, bleak and lonely.

She felt a storm was coming – the pressure on her head was getting heavier. The clouds were darkening in the North East. Rain mingled with the tears on her face. She tightened the shawl round her swelling body. She shivered, not only because of the briskening wind but also from fear of sailors' ghosts, lured to their deaths by Wreckers who once stood on this shore in bad weather with lamps, making it look like a safe harbour to ships.

Where could she find refuge from the storm that was coming to her? She looked back at the gloomy Martello fortress – her mother was right - there was nothing for it but the Workhouse.

Eliza walked to Wickham Market a few miles away, to enter the Workhouse and await the birth of her child. The workhouse - the cold comfort final resort; unmarried pregnant women who had begun "to show" went there and did domestic work while awaiting their babies. They stayed there the minimum time they could. It made no difference if they were victims of sexual violence, incest, had been kept mistresses or had lived with men who subsequently abandoned them. Their stories would not be believed or even heard in the workhouse or the street where they found themselves.

Needing a quiet place where she could rest and think, she instead had to go into this feared of all places - "The Bastille" folk called it - there to start at once a life of austere routine, to begin her reformation. Grieving all she had lost; her hopes ended by painful rejection, she toiled up the hill, past the spire of All Saints Church which folks said looked down on thirty other churches. Then she saw it for the first time, the huge forbidding brick building dominating the skyline - the Union Workhouse.

The High Street of the ancient town was busy with shops, inns and businesses. Walking along the old Roman road, she saw the decayed post of the Potsford Gibbet still standing. White Georgian houses grouped around the market square with its parish pump. A timber framed manor house and a yellow brick house flanked the other side where the road descended down to the River. Here there was a watermill, its great waterwheel turning by the bridge. A basket maker was working nearby.

But Eliza didn't take much notice of this. As she approached the massive wrought iron gates of the workhouse, the porter came out, unlocked them and let her through. He took her to the lodge, where he entered the time, name and sex of every person arriving or departing in neat copperplate writing in his ledger. He said with a grin,

"It's easier to get out of hell than it is to leave the workhouse without a pass."

Eliza shuddered. She noticed that the entry above hers read "8am; departure of hearse with female corpse for burial."

After admitting her, the porter rang a bell and a woman came in, who introduced herself as "Miss Sharp" and asked her: "Are you really homeless and destitute? - we'll soon find out if you're hiding anything. You will be stripped, searched and your hair cropped. If I find anything of value, it will be sold to help pay for your keep." Eliza gasped. She was glad she had left Freddie's ring behind with Mother at home for safekeeping. The woman handed Eliza a card of rules and snapped,

"Follow me, Stone."

The main building had rows of bare windows. Eliza was shocked at the grimness of the place - it was like a prison. She followed Miss Sharp through a large oak door that creaked as it opened. Inside was a high gloomy corridor painted dark green half the way up the walls. Eliza's spirits plummeted further. It was bleak and bitterly cold. Their footsteps echoed as they walked. The place smelt of stale food, old clothes and sickness.

Miss Sharp took her to Matron's office. This lady wore an ankle-length dark blue dress with broad white starched cuffs; a white apron, thick dark stockings and lace-up shoes. Her hair was completely covered with a starched white square of cloth which fell in a triangular shape at the back of her head.

Seeing that Eliza was pregnant, she agreed to admit her to the receiving ward, saying, "Men, women and children are segregated here. The medical officer will see you tomorrow morning. Now your clothes must be disinfested and you will have a bath." The bathhouse was freezing cold with dark tiles on the walls and a stone flagged floor. It was lit by a single gas bracket high up on the wall. There were four baths and a row of basins on a long wooden trestle.

Miss Sharp picked up her scissors and grabbed hold of her hair. Eliza tried to pull away from her, but the warden hissed "It's to stop the spread of lice, it's got to be done". Then she watched scornfully as Eliza shivered in a few inches of lukewarm water and tried to wash herself with a bar of soap that wouldn't lather. After handing her a threadbare towel, Miss Sharp bundled her clothes up to be fumigated - and gave her coarse underwear that felt scratchy, a prison- style uniform of grey dress and white apron with a striped blanket shawl and black boots that didn't fit.

Eliza felt humiliated and vulnerable. She felt she must have done something very wrong to end up in this place. Miss Sharp informed her that her clothes, comb and handkerchief would be washed and labelled and that she would get them back when she left. "The medical officer will inspect and classify you tomorrow and then you will go to the dormitories in the main building. Able- bodied women go to the ground floor right at the end, near the kitchen. Women's exercise yards are at the front of the building near the privies."

The receiving ward was overcrowded with people, who had been through the same process, waiting to be admitted to the workhouse. The vagrants staying overnight went to the casual ward where they slept and had a meal, in return for four hours work the next morning. The small dormitory was crammed with rough hessian bags filled with straw, thin grey blankets and lumpy pillows on the floor. It was difficult to sleep through the snuffling and snoring of the other women. Eliza was anxious and slept badly till the early morning light woke her. Somewhere a loud bell was clanging. The other women were stirring. It was time to get up.

She submitted passively to the medical officer's inspection. Once more compelled to be naked in front of a stranger with Matron standing in the background. He examined her intimately and felt her stomach. She felt like an animal and grew hot with embarrassment. He spoke curtly to her, "When you get nearer your time - I estimate it will be in the early spring - you will have light duties. For now you are fit to work and can take your turn in the laundry and kitchen."

The laundry was a vast, noisy room, full of steam and the smell of soapsuds. Several women were slaving over large tubs where the clothes were washed, their red faces shiny with sweat. The bleach stung Eliza's eyes and condensation ran down the windows and puddled on the floor. They pulled heavy wooden racks down from the high ceiling, draped the sheets and clothes over them then hoisted them up to the ceiling where they dripped on to the women toiling below. The wet things were heavy and Eliza's hands were sore with scrubbing so she was relieved when it was time for dinner. Breakfast had been a piece of bread and a bowl of gruel - thin porridge with treacle.

The dining room contained a couple of dozen benches alongside bare trestle tables all facing the same way, set with a motley collection of cutlery. It stank of stale food despite the two open windows, which were covered with whitewash making the room dark. The walls were bare except for two large boards. One had `GOD IS TRUTH` written on it and the other 'GOD IS GOOD'. One of the tables had a pair of brass scales on it, because it was standard practice that any inmate might ask to have his rations weighed. Eliza doubted if anyone would dare to challenge the Master.

Dinner was bread and cheese. Meat or bacon and vegetables were only provided on two days a week and once a week they had soup and bread. Supper, when it came after more back- breaking work, was bread and cheese again, every day of the week. She thought of the meals in the servant's hall – the abundance of delicious food, the gossip and chat with her friends - and blinked back the tears. Most of the women were old and had been living there for a long time. She tried to talk to them but they seemed too frightened and anyway, knowing nothing of life outside, they had nothing to talk about, and were afraid of being reported to the Master and punished if they complained. Most were worn down by drudgery and the monotonous life.

At break time, the women were allowed outside into the exercise yard. Eliza went down some steps and found a courtyard with high walls topped by iron railings and a pump where the women lined up to drink. Other women walked around with heads down and shoulders hunched. Eliza looked round, half hoping, half dreading to see anyone she knew in this terrible place. The grass was patchy and there were no trees or seats, just a wide stone path round the edge for wet weather. This was the only time that the children over eighteen months old saw their mothers. They were allowed to come in and join them. Mrs. Sharp was always on duty, looking out for bad behaviour. Some women looked up at the windows of the men's day room where the men waved at them and mouthed greetings. A handbell was rung from one of the lower windows and the women drifted back to their workplaces.

That night, Eliza slept in the able bodied women's dormitory - it was cold with just a few dead coals in the fireplace and twenty truckle beds with a wooden chair beside each one. The floor and walls were bare, but the two large windows were open. She could hardly get warm under the worn blanket and cried herself to sleep.

At the next Guardians' Meeting, Eliza stood before a row of complacent, plump gentlemen who sat at the other side of a long table. Most of them were farmers and the main employers in the area. They had a vested interest in keeping wages low and the Poor Rate under control. She recognised the medical officer and thought that the gentleman in the dark suit, starched white collar with waistcoat and watch chain who exuded authority, must be the Master who lived in the large house at the end of the building. A tall thin bespectacled man took charge of the meeting. He tapped on the table to bring everyone to order. Then he turned his attention to Eliza.

"How did you come to present yourself at the workhouse door?"

She hung her head in shame and said "I've been sacked from my job as housemaid at De Vere Hall, Sir, for being pregnant. There is no room or money to keep me at home." She didn't mention Freddie, just as the mistress had instructed her. The board members murmured among themselves.

"Well, you had better admit her, Master. She has been very foolish to behave so badly and lose such a good post. We all know of Lord De Vere and he's a very good employer. We'll review the situation when she has been delivered of her child - another mouth for the parish to feed, I shouldn't wonder." Eliza was stung into a reply.

"No, Sir, my parents have agreed to look after the child and I shall leave here as soon as possible and find work."

"Good thing too, as long as you've paid your bill

here, of course. You may go, Stone."

On her way back to the laundry, Eliza heard the screams of a woman who was being dragged along and then shut in an empty room. Later she heard that she had concealed a few turnips thrown into the Yard by her sister on her way to admission. Discipline was tight and inmates were locked up for any insolence or disobedience, or even flogged for more serious misconduct.

All the inmates had to attend the Sunday service in the chapel with the chaplain. Many people slept through the service which lasted an hour. There was no music or singing of hymns to lift Eliza's spirits, because most people could not read. The sermon was based on the biblical text 'WHEN LUST HATH CONCEIVED, IT BRINGETH FORTH SIN' James 1.15. Eliza prayed that God would forgive her and take pity on her poor baby. It wasn't lust but love which had brought her here.

She found that the able-bodied women were mostly widows with children or unmarried mothers like herself. There were a few vagrants. Single women with bastard children were required to have their meals separately from the other women paupers to avoid contaminating their morals. Eliza found their conversation coarse. "Why didn't you get rid of the baby with a knitting needle, have hot baths, drink gin or fall down stairs?" One girl asked her. "You can eat the lead from plasters or make up some "hickey pickey" - bitter apple, aloes and white lead - "a penny each from the chemist, love". The thought of it made Eliza feel sick. "Got dismissed, did ya? Catch me hevin some rich man's bastard. Hey - it wasn't the master was it?" They laughed and all burst into a chorus of,

> It's the same the whole world over,
> It's the poor wot gets the blame,
> It's the rich wot gets the pleasures
> Ain't it all a bleedin' shame?"

Sometimes, they would talk to her about giving birth. "Are you scared, dear?" one said. She knew she faced a dangerous, painful and unpleasant time. She was completely unprepared for the birth. Her mother hid her bulge under her voluminous skirt and petticoat. Her babies were born at home but Eliza knew nothing about it. She was sent out of the house for the delivery and when she came back, father told her she had another brother or sister.

She tried to keep the fear to herself, knowing that other women got over it, not once but many times. She was now consigned to jobs where she could sit down; preparing vegetables, patching blankets and picking oakum, right up until the day the baby was born. Oakum was the worst work - it meant picking the tarred ends of rope into separate strands with blunt and bleeding nails so they could be sold to shipyards to be jammed into cracks in the wooden hulls.

She hoped for a good night's sleep but the pains began as soon as she went to bed. The other women complained about her moaning and sent for the nurse who helped her walk to the infirmary. The baby wasn't born for another twenty four hours, during which the attendant did nothing to help her suffering, except to say "It will get much worse - this is nothing." She gazed round the room in despair. It smelled strongly of disinfectant which failed to cover the stink of urine, sickness and stained mattresses. There were ten beds with patients in various states of discomfort and disarray; some tightly wrapped in the blankets, others had thrown off their covering and lay exposed in dirty nightgowns. The chamber pots beneath the beds needed emptying. The nurse was merely an inmate who had been promoted to save the expense of paying a proper nurse. She was sitting at the far side of the room knitting and rarely bothered to look up.

Eliza's pains were still bearable, then she felt a gush of warm water and they got a bit stronger and closer together. The longer pains made her catch her breath. She breathed deeply and it made her feel better. Matron came in and felt the bump all over. She fixed old sheets torn into long rags on to the bed posts, "To pull on when the time comes". She instructed the nurse to fetch boiling water. Eliza lost track of time. She heard a voice saying, "Lie still!" and they gave her some gin to ease the pain and keep her quiet. There were long deep thrusting pains. Eliza shouted: "I want to push!"

Matron felt again between her legs. "Next time you can" Eliza felt she might split in half. First the head came out, then one shoulder then the other. She heard a wail. "It's a girl". She held her baby while Matron cut the cord. Nurse took the baby away to wash her, then washed Eliza with water from a big enamel basin. The baby cried and nurse swaddled her and gave her to

Eliza to feed. As she looked into those dark blue eyes, a wave of love came over her and she was amazed how much the baby seemed to know already. Nurse raised an eyebrow and cocked her head at Matron, "Has it come to stay?" she asked, "Oh, yes, she's strong that one, more's the pity. She and her mother are an abomination against nature and living proof of fornication. Sin and disease will be passed down in "bad blood" and hang in the air infecting others."

They put the baby in its cot. Eliza felt so happy she took no notice of them, turned over with a sigh and fell into an exhausted sleep. Outside the birds were singing - spring had come and, even in the workhouse, a baby brought joy. She was determined to get well as soon as possible and go home. As soon as the lying-in period was over she would get away from this awful place. She would call the baby Freda or Fredericka, something to remind her of Freddie, "There, there, my little darling, I've got you," she crooned as she breastfed her.

The girl in the next bed died in the night. In the dirty conditions, she'd been infected by another patient on the ward suffering from puerperal fever. Infant mortality was high- one in six babies died - and illegitimate babies were twice as likely to die in the first year. No wonder many people believed you came out worse than you went in, but it was the only resort if serious illness struck and you had no money and nowhere else to go. At least it was better than having the baby in a ditch and she was away from the prying eyes of neighbours and relatives. She wondered what Frederick would think of the baby - she already had his dark hair and she was so beautiful. She remembered that the Baron had flown into a rage when he found out what happened. Hopefully he had not cut him off without a penny as she had heard him threatening to do. Poor Frederick would have to earn his own living if that happened. She thought of his soft sensitive hands and shook her head.

But why should she worry about him when she and the baby were in this terrible place wondering what would become of them and even if they would survive? Now she thought of the rich pampered aristocrats living in luxury in their big houses far away from the harsh reality of poor people's lives. Exploiting the poor and reaping the profit from their endless toil.

She knew the London season would be starting soon and Freddie and his family would go up to London; to live in their town house, so that they could attend all the balls, dinner parties and sporting events of the summer. Marianne, the youngest, would be presented at court with the other debutantes of the year who had reached their eighteenth birthday.

Eliza had seen pictures of these girls in the papers and knew they wore white gowns embellished with layers of lace, long white gloves; their hair piled up on top of their heads, crowned with three Prince of Wales ostrich feathers. She had read an article describing the long queue of carriages waiting outside Buckingham Palace. There they would pass through gorgeous state rooms while they waited to be presented to Queen Victoria and curtsey low before her Majesty. A daughter of a Peer, like Marianne, received a royal kiss on the cheek, while other girls were merely allowed to kiss the Queen's hand.

She knew that no expense would be spared for the coming out ball, with a marquee in the garden, the sound of champagne corks popping floating out over the gardens; flowers everywhere - carnations and lilies of the valley on the supper tables, white roses in the hall. Musicians, Dukes and Duchesses - beautiful waltzes, gaiety and perfume would fill the air. And at the end of it all, maybe, an engagement to an earl!

How different was her life to that of these privileged girls!

But she was glad when she was able to get up and leave the lying- in ward, the noisiest and worst behaved part of the workhouse. There were some young girls in their teens, like her, with their first baby, victims of their own simplicity, duped by men who took advantage of their trusting nature, but most were regulars with a lifetime of prostitution behind them. Quarrelling and fighting often broke out and they were resentful and uncooperative with the staff. Many were alcoholics and fought with knives or fists at the slightest provocation. The nurses muttered to each other that they were "a disagreeable lot - bad-tempered and repulsive".

She looked out of the window and watched a horse ambulance being admitted at the large iron gates. Cries of pain or moans could be heard; pauper lunatics worked in the gardens; ragged families trailed up the drive; when there was a funeral, the coffin, a plain deal box, was taken by horse and cart to the workhouse cemetery; in the morning, the workhouse children were escorted to the local Board school in a long crocodile, all wearing the same drab clothes, the girls with unbleached calico aprons. Now and then an inmate would come out and be greeted by friends or relations at the gate; sometimes there would be no one and they would wonder away alone.

The day finally came when she too could leave. The debt was paid and she was given a pass by the Porter - she had got out of hell! She breathed in deeply, savouring the fresh morning air. Oh it was good to be out in the open, to be free. She was wearing her own clothes; it was wonderful to feel soft underwear against her skin and have her own dress and shawl. She'd lost weight and her clothes hung loosely on her now. Even her hair had grown again. She shook off the oppression of those thick walls and iron gates, the damp and cold of the workhouse. She felt like a bird set free. Clasping her baby to her, bundled in her shawl, she set off across the road to where her father was waiting for her.

And so they climbed up into the trap and set off for home. She had written home to tell them the news when the baby was born.

Chapter Five - A Lady Visits

Eliza came home from the workhouse clutching her new baby daughter to her breast, wrapped in her black shawl to keep out the early March wind. She was still dazed from her experiences in the infirmary and glad to reach the comparative peace and comfort of her parents' cottage after the noise and smell of the public lying-in ward. All she could think of as she walked past the curious gaze of the neighbours was that she would have to give up her precious child in a few weeks.

Her mother hugged her and the baby but soon began to complain

"I suppose I'm going to have to look after her when you go. Liza, I'm too old for all this now - me and your father, and we've still got a houseful."

"I'm sorry, Mother" Eliza said, tears starting to prick her eyes. She sank wearily down into a battered armchair in the front room.

"Leave off, Mother," said her father stumping into the room. Can't you see the girl's tired? She's been shamed enough at the Workhouse. You girls'll help won't you?"

Her younger sisters, Maud and Rose, gathered round eagerly to see the baby. "Oh, yes. What a little dear. Isn't she beautiful! What a lot of hair she's got."

Eliza fed the baby. Afterwards they put her in a drawer, lined with a blanket, to sleep. The girls were fascinated by the child and pleased to have a new sister.

That evening, Mother sat beside Eliza while she

hemmed small flannel gowns and linen sheets. Eliza said, "I'm sorry for bringing disgrace on the family and more hard work to you mother."

"Well, it's no use crying over spilt milk - what's done is done - we must be practical about the future. We must do what we can for her - it's better than the workhouse and she is one of us. We take care of our own - no one will go without, if I can help it - look at your grandfather over there - he's happy enough." They looked over at Granpa's chair and seeing that he was asleep again, they smiled at each other. Their nosy neighbour, of course couldn't resist hurrying over to see the new baby.

"What a lovely little thing. However can anyone say such as her ought not to be born? She's a beauty. They say, you know, that that sort of child is the finest."

Eliza took the back- handed compliments with a wry smile and thanked her.

Maudie went to the rectory to fetch the Baby Box which the Rector's daughter always filled with things to lend to new babies in the village. Eliza was delighted with the pink flowered print frocks, tiny shirts, nighties and napkins. She unpacked a packet of tea and sugar, groats for gruel and was pleased with the loan of a baby bath. This kind lady also brought Eliza a sago pudding, veal broth and half a pint of stout a day to build up her strength.

A few days later they heard the sound of wheels and horses' hooves outside the cottage. A chaise was pulling up at the gate. The driver jumped down and helped a lady out of the carriage. She wore a blue silk gown, jacket and blue bonnet. Mother got up and opened the door as the lady lifted the latch on the gate and proceeded down the path towards her. "This is the house of Eliza Stone is it not?"

"Yes, my Lady." Mother bobbed a curtsey.

"And you are her mother?" The visitor inquired. She was tall and dark with imperious good looks. "I've come to see the child - where is she?"

She had to lower her head to enter the tiny cottage and exclaimed loudly, "Oh, it's so cramped in here!" Her eyes examined the room as she sat down, uninvited, with her skirts billowing around her. Eliza came in, surprised, straightening her dress,

"Miss De Vere, we are honoured by your visit. Have you come to see the baby?"

"Indeed, I have," Cecelia De Vere sniffed. "Where is it? Oh, it's not kept in that drawer is it? It must have a proper cot." The baby sneezed and Cecilia softened somewhat in her manner.

"I feel it is my duty to make sure she is properly cared for, after all she is family, of a sort - I have something for you" - she handed a little bag of sovereigns to Mother, who took it eagerly, realising there could be some advantages in the situation after all – it's an ill wind that does nobody any good, she thought.

"She will be called Bertha Helen" Cecelia said, "family names of ours. When you register the birth, leave the father's name blank. My brother has his position in society to uphold and his reputation cannot be compromised. His indiscretions must not be made known. In return for secrecy we offer financial

83

support. I think you will agree this will be best for both parties. My father has been informed and we will take care of everything. Eliza herself should leave the area as soon as possible - those are the terms on which I will give her a reference. Of course she must never again contact Frederick. He has just returned from a visit to our West Indies estates. We hope he will eventually make a suitable marriage and have a legitimate heir." She cocked an enquiring eyebrow at Eliza, who nodded dumbly. So that was why Freddie had not come after her, she thought.

"Good. Now I must go, I have other calls to make, but I shall come again to see how she's getting along. My eldest sister, Adeline, is busy with the preparations for her forthcoming wedding to Colonel Blake. I will be taking over her duties as father's hostess and household manager. Good day."

Mother opened the door for her and she swept out.

Eliza went over to the baby. She cooed "There, there, my little indiscretion - seems like you're going to be a lady." She knew that going away was for her own good. She could make a new start, find work, maybe marry and have children one day. She had wanted to stay nearby, but this would be a better life for the baby.

Six weeks later, when she went to register the birth, Eliza duly withheld the father's name and occupation as had been agreed. The registrar asked, "Do you want to seek an affiliation order from the magistrate? You could get five shillings a week."

"No - thank you, the child is well provided for." She thought that, in this case, the magistrate had good reason to avoid the case coming to court!

"Just, as long as she doesn't become a charge on the Parish."

"No, Sir."

Eliza had a certain pride in the secret identity of the father. She felt that her association with this great family was a source of kudos. Her child had a benefactor and protector far better than other men; she was related to the aristocracy - high born, even though illegitimate. She herself had been dispossessed of what she had dreamed - but her child had her birthright, nothing could take that from her. They had even chosen her names. They acknowledged her as family. Eliza hoped they would look after her and not break their word as Freddie had broken his promise to her.

Back home in Pump Square, Eliza gave her baby all the love she could while she still had her near; breast feeding her until she was old enough to wean. She followed her mother's example and kept Bertha in bed with her for warmth, in spite of Miss De Vere's leaflet about the risk of mothers rolling over and suffocating the child. At six weeks, the baby went on to bread and milk and gradually onto solid food. Eliza knew that soon she would have to give her beloved daughter up. It was best to pass the baby to her parents to bring up as their own child, give up her rights as a parent and find work and a new life elsewhere, visiting her in the role of sister, when she could. This way Bertha would have a normal home and family life.

Eliza felt lucky her parents had agreed to help. She

knew other girls in her situation went out to work as servants and paid for the child to be boarded out with strangers who left them to die, neglected and malnourished. Some single mothers even became so desperate they were driven to infanticide. Miss De Vere visited them regularly, distributing advice, disinfectants and religious tracts. She told them to keep their house cleaner but the dirt was caused by bad sanitation and poverty. It was cheaper and quicker to blame mother's incompetence than to begin long term and costly improvements.

After the six weeks, which was her grieving time, Eliza, had to face up to parting from her precious child; she dressed her and fed her for the last time then handed her to her mother. She must go away alone to start her new job. Miserable and broken hearted, she turned at the door of the cottage.

"I'm afraid Bertha will think I didn't love her and abandoned her. I don't want her to think badly of me because of what I've done."

"She won't think that if I've got anything to do with it. Go on, now, it's best for all of us," urged her mother, pushing her out of the door.

Eliza arrived in Ipswich in answer to an advertisement she had noticed in the East Anglian Daily Times for "domestic servant for a doctor." She was amazed at the size of the county town she saw around her. She had never seen so many people and houses crowded together. She read signs for iron foundries making farm machinery and railway parts, brick works, cement making. There were also printing, fertiliser, tobacco and cloth factories. She noticed the masts of ships in the port towering above the roof tops - their sails partially unfurled to dry in the sun, unloading cargoes of wheat and barley.

The port and waterfront were busy and ships were moored from other British ports and transporting goods from Ipswich. Shipbuilding flourished.

The town had gas lighting, a police force, a museum and a fine corn exchange. The town hall looked new. Horse drawn trams clattered down the streets and she read a sign outside the public Park that it had once been the grounds of Christchurch Mansion.

As she walked along the crowded streets, it was good to be anonymous, lost among a crowd of strangers who knew nothing about her past. Near the docks, she saw prostitutes calling out to the men passers-by and felt how nearly she too could have been reduced to this, if her parents had not taken Bertha in and the De Veres had not given her a reference. Domestic work was the only job she could do, she had no other skills and not much education. People looked down on servants but at least it was respectable and prepared you for marriage and maybe, one day, children of your own that you could love and keep.

The advertisement had said "Good general servant required for doctor's house (country girl preferred); small washing; cook kept; age not over 35 - write, stating age, wage and full particulars to Mrs. Green." Eliza had written and was now summoned to interview, dressed in her best dress, jacket and hat. The address given led her to a substantial Georgian townhouse. The entrance doorway was completed by a graceful pediment resting on detached columns. Sash windows were arranged in balanced order in the brickwork and painted white.

She rang the doorbell and as she entered the paved hall, she saw a fine staircase with carved wooden newel posts and banisters. She glimpsed living rooms furnished with large panels of painted wood. There was a prevailing lightness and delicacy carried on by the doorways and window surrounds, chimney pieces and plastered ceilings. She was shown into the study where she noticed through the window, shady lawns, gardens divided by alleyways and hedges where flowers bloomed among knots and parterres beside stone ornaments and in the distance, peaches ripening on a sunny wall.

Mrs. Green, a gaunt, imposing woman, surveyed her dispassionately. "Sit down, girl, that's it - are you from the country? Good - I find village girls more obedient than town girls - the last one I had was impertinent. You look clean. A church goer? Regular habits? Early riser? Schooled in household chores? Now why did you leave your last employment?"

To all the previous questions, Eliza had nodded her head and said, "Yes, Ma'am" but now she hesitated, before coming out with a well-rehearsed lie, "My mother was ill and so I had to go home and take care of her."

"Indeed? I trust she is now well and you won't be asking for more time away?"

"Oh, no, Ma'am, she is quite well."

Mrs. Green, settled down into her chair again and took a deep breath, "Well, you have good references, I shall take you on. I prefer an attractive well-spoken girl. You realise we have only one other indoor servant - we live quietly here, not like the people at De Vere Hall." she allowed a small smile to soften her lips. "And by the way, I always call my parlour maids Dorothy."

Eliza didn't mind what she was called, she was grateful for the work. And she did work - Mrs. Green certainly got her money's worth. She rose at six in summer, half past six in winter; swept and dusted the drawing room, and dining room before breakfast; took tea up for the Master and Mistress and carried water up for their baths. After having her own breakfast, she made her bed and swept and dusted the front staircase. Because she was required to act as a parlour maid during the day, once she had finished her chores, she put on a clean cap and apron when bringing in the family breakfast. Then she rushed upstairs to make the beds.

Before luncheon she dressed in her black merino wool dress with white cap, apron and cuffs. She had to answer the door to callers, clear luncheon and wash the glasses and silver. In the afternoon she did needlework, then prepared the tea, carried it into the parlour and cleared away afterwards. In the evening she laid the table for dinner and waited on the family. Mrs. Green taught her how to serve the food and wine correctly; food from the left hand side and wine from the right. Eliza felt the job was a step up for her as she was doing the work of a footman or butler, with direct contact with the family. She was tall enough to reach over the table and moved gracefully about the room, told never to react to the conversation at table. She acted as lady's maid to Mrs. Green, helping her with dressing. It was also her job to clean and trim the lamps used in the sitting room and get up the fine linen of the family.

Eliza kept the pantry clean and in order, closed the shutters before dinner and lit the lamps in the sitting room, corridor and hall as soon as it was dusk. Then after dinner, she again made a round of the bedrooms and put them in order, lit fires in the bedrooms in the evenings if required, turned down the beds, filled the jugs with hot water, finally closing the curtains. She was so busy that she didn't have time to think and at night she fell into an exhausted sleep.

Mrs. Green said "Now Dorothy, I'm most particular about visitors being kept waiting on the doorstep, especially as most of them are patients, paying customers of the doctor. Open the door promptly and show them into the waiting room, politely. I do not receive many visitors myself and I will tell you if I am "at home" or not, to callers, in the morning. Sometimes I am engaged in domestic matters or going through the accounts and in this case, you must take the visitor's card, if offered or receive a message with a courteous, "Yes, Ma'am".

It was Cook's job to answer the door from ten to twelve so that Eliza could get on with her housework. Eliza noticed her putting her head through the window, or looking up the area steps, checking who it was before trudging upstairs to answer the door. Ugly or suspicious-looking people she called from her vantage point to find out their business. Eliza worried that some time passed before Cook could pull down her sleeves, change her apron, wash her face and hands and open the door.

Tradesmen called at the area or back-door in any case; the milkman, baker, butcher, fishmonger and the greengrocer. Many street traders came round the houses with their horse and carts; the muffin man ringing his bell, the rag and bone man and the scrap iron man calling out. So Cook was hot and flustered enough in the mornings; after attending to the family breakfast, she made out the menu for the day's dinner and luncheon on a slate according to the contents of the larder; then she had to take it to the mistress and consult with her about any changes for the day. Mrs. Green would make suggestions or take the opportunity to praise or criticize her cooking. Eliza always crossed her fingers this last wouldn't happen as it meant Cook would be banging about in the kitchen, slamming saucepans and threatening to leave, until Eliza sat her down, got her a nice cup of tea and reassured her.

Then Cook got on with the soup for the next day. Eliza watched her make the jellies, creams, entrees and finally the luncheon. The afternoon was Cook's time off, except on the rare occasion when there was a dinner party or when guests were staying in the house when there was naturally more work to be done. She usually had a nap. Five o'clock to nine in the evening was always a busy time for her and Eliza.

Fortunately, the family enjoyed plain cooking and they had provided a modern Kitchener range to cook on. Cook had clearing up and dish washing to do after dinner. Then, last thing, she would see that the doors and windows of the basement were secured and the kitchen fire burnt low, before retiring for the night at about ten o'clock.

As well as the indoor staff, there was a gardener/groom called Henry, who worked outside and looked after the small garden and the pony and carriage used by the doctor for his house calls. Henry grew fruit, flowers and vegetables for the house. Cook always reminded him "leave your muddy boots outside when you come into my clean kitchen, Henry."

Eliza missed the friends she'd left behind. She remembered the stables and stud farm at the De Vere estate and the head gardener with his big staff; how he objected to his choicest blooms being cut by the mistress, the finest bunch of grapes being gathered, or his Paxton's Peach cases being rifled. He insisted on picking these himself and his autocratic rule was tolerated as a mark of the high esteem the Baron had for him.

Still, she mustn't think of the past, she must get on with her work. And yet when she was alone in her little attic room at night she would hold Bertha's shawl, and rock herself back and forth, longing for her baby in her arms. She had to go on living and working even though her heart felt numb. There was an invisible tie that bound her to her baby; whatever she did, wherever she went. She missed her every day, every minute of the day - she was always at the back of her mind. She sent her presents but that didn't fill the gap inside her. She went through life like a machine now because life had stopped when she had left Bertha. She kept the weight of guilt and painful memories deep down inside where they would not trouble her. She tried to believe that it hadn't really happened. She had no one she could talk to about it anyway, so she kept it close. Mrs. Green would sack her if she found out she was an immoral woman. At just twenty years old, she looked older, a beautiful girl with sadness in her eyes. She wrote to her mother: -

"How is Bertha? Has she settled down alright without me? Is she feeding and sleeping well? She's such a lovely baby and I have so many memories of her. Thank you for looking after her, I can never repay your kindness. Maybe one day I will be able to take care of her myself, when I get settled. I will come and see you all as soon as I can, but I don't get much time off and I'm so far away."

In the afternoons, Henry, in his groom's livery of well-cut breeches, trim gaiters and hunting stock, drove the doctor out in the carriage to make home visits to patients. Sometimes he acted as Mrs. Green's footman, when she paid her calls. These gave her a social life and established suitable contacts for the doctor which might lead to his advantage. Henry told Eliza and Cook

"I have to enquire if the person on whom she was calling is at home. If not "at home," I leave her card for the mistress of the house, and the doctor's for both the mistress and her husband. From three pm to six pm, each visit lasts only fifteen minutes of polite conversation and Mrs. Green gets to three or four houses a day. To save me having to climb down from my box, I hail a passing boy and ask him to ring the door-bell. I point with my whip to the one in question. Instead of having to persuade street boys who are very

93

cheeky and much given to backchat, I prefer to call a delivery boy with a basket, as they are more biddable. I tell him "Just you ring that bell, there's a good lad! Pull it hard please."

He explained that sometimes the old girl would lose patience and get out and ring the bell herself, rather than wait around. Eliza new what she was like, as she spent much time helping Mrs. Green change her clothes in order to be correctly dressed for every occasion. This was her only exercise, going for a drive.

One morning, Henry brought in fresh flowers from the garden in the early morning and started arranging them on the table. "Those are lovely", Eliza said, setting the tea tray to take up to the doctor and mistress. He was pleased and tried to be friendly but she was wary now of relationships and kept her distance. She had been so hurt in the past she just wanted to do her work and get through the days. Henry seemed to understand and respected her wishes.

Adversity could have diminished Eliza, but in time she grew strong, independent and sensitive to the needs and feelings of others. She gradually regained her optimism, cheerfulness and ability to talk to anyone anywhere. One morning in April, she saw a newspaper lying on the kitchen table and read about her former Mistress at De Vere Hall. The headline announced; "Miss Adeline De Vere, eldest daughter of Baron De Vere, marries Colonel Lewis Blake, eldest son of a banker of Kings Lynn, Norfolk, at Campsie Ash Church. Eliza remembered the party at the hall held to celebrate the engagement last year. How different her life was then, when she was in love with Freddie. She read on with interest. "The bride wore a white silk dress with long sleeves and a generous train of lace. She carried a bouquet of Maiden Blush roses and wore a long veil, surmounted by a wreath of roses and orange blossom. The couple were greeted by cheering crowds of villagers and tenants." There was a photograph showing the bride looking modest and feminine, hanging on the bridegroom's arm. Eliza put down the paper with a sigh. Frederick would have been there.

She daydreamed. Soon he would be leaving the Hall with the rest of the family and travelling up to London for the three months' Season as they did every year. Lord De Vere would take his seat in the House of Commons while the family lived at their townhouse in a fashionable part of London. Freddie and his sisters would enjoy lavish balls, dinners, and theatre, as well as the round of social events; Henley Regatta, Glyndebourne, the Royal Academy Art Exhibition, Ascot races and Lords Test match; Eton versus Harrow. The Hall closed down in mid- April and most of the servants were put on board wages while carriages and horses, grooms, footmen, butler and the head housekeeper with her chosen minions went up to London. Eliza had heard all about it in the servants' hall last year. She wished she were going with them.

Chapter Six - A New Beginning

Eliza learned that her employer, Dr. Green, was also the medical officer for Ipswich Workhouse. She thought he looked very smart in his black frock coat, white linen shirt with stiff cravat, blue waistcoat and boots as she handed him his top hat and cane. He left the house carrying the black bag containing all his instruments.

He had qualified as a doctor and become a General Practitioner after a distinguished career in the Navy and flung himself into caring for the health of paupers with enthusiasm and courage. Mrs. Green disapproved, although he received a fee for this and preferred him to spend more time with his rich patients. He was constantly improving the conditions at the workhouse: stoves were installed in the Probationary Wards to warm paupers coming from the bathroom and the diet of the youngest children and the sick in the infirmary was better.

During an outbreak of small pox in the area he ordered the vaccination of all new inmates, however some had already contracted the disease - one woman died of it leaving an infant and because of the great fear of infection, the funeral had to be carried out at night in the workhouse burial ground.

He was much respected by the Board and great friends with the Master, who was also the schoolmaster. He would often find him with several boys in the schoolroom, reading stories to them or helping them to draw animals. They were also allowed to bathe in the river, and join the parish choir.

Eliza was constantly answering the doorbell to a stream of patients calling at the house to ask for the doctor's help and advice. The surgery was a downstairs room, where the patients visited at set times of the day to discuss their symptoms. Those who couldn't afford the doctor's fee went to the apothecary for remedies or the local wise woman who grew herbs in her garden and knew their healing power. The doctor understood medicines but did not mix them, and knew enough surgery to get by - if the case was complicated, the surgeon was called in. There were many diseases; frequent cases of cholera, bronchitis and TB. Eliza often heard the doctor say

"House drainage, water supplies and general sanitation in this town are criminally dangerous for public safety."

Despite his best efforts, the passing bell often proclaimed that someone in the parish lay on his death bed, and then after the death, the bell tolled for each year of the person's life. Funerals, with the women in black and the men wearing armbands were frequent. People wore mourning clothes for many months when someone in their family had died.

Neither did the good doctor have a remedy for what troubled Eliza. Pale and sick at heart, she needed help and humanity to heal her loss. She couldn't forget Bertha and longed to see her again. Her mother wrote to say that the baby was doing well, contented and happy. Eliza was pleased and hoped her mother would be able to manage, with her younger sisters' help and the De Veres' money. She didn't want the baby to suffer for her wrongdoing. It was a comfort to her that she was able to send money towards Bertha's upkeep.

When she did manage to get home, it was wonderful to hold the baby in her arms again and hear Rose and Maud talking excitedly about all the progress she was making but sad that she had missed so much. She saw the baby reaching out for her grandmother and growing to love her sisters more than her. This hurt, as did knowing she couldn't claim the child as her own. Would she always be a distant figure in Bertha's life? At least she wasn't left in the workhouse or being brought up by strangers. There was much to be thankful for and she must just take advantage of the opportunity she had been given to make a new life; to work, find acceptance and respect and one day perhaps to marry and have a babies of her own to love and care for.

No one would know she wasn't pure as the driven snow, a respectable, pure woman, as long as she kept her secret. She was aware no working man could or would take on the burden of a child that was not his own - he would have enough of a struggle bringing up his own family, and might think such a child had inherited the "bad blood" of its mother. He would surely hate this evidence that his wife had had a sexual relationship with another man. And it would be condoning immorality.

Perhaps it was inevitable that sooner or later, being so close to the Hall, she should meet Freddie again, coming across the fields near the village. He was striding along swishing at the ripe corn with his cane. She tried to pass by but he caught her arm and insisted on speaking to her.

"Eliza, I must talk to you, to explain what happened."

"No need," she shook her head, "I heard all about it from your sister, Cecelia. She came and laid down the law, so we all know where we stand."

"You mustn't mind her too much. She means well, she's been trained to visit the poor from childhood. She feels it's her duty."

"Yes, at least your family owe us that."

He went on. "Please forgive me, Eliza, I never meant to hurt you."

"It's all in the past now. I've put it behind me," she replied.

He tried to put his arm around her, to comfort her.

"No, don't touch me," she shook him off angrily, though her whole being longed for him. "Haven't you done me enough harm already?"

"Eliza, I'm not able to marry who I love. Father wants me to marry an heiress or the daughter of an Earl, like Mother." He appealed to her.

"I understand that - now" she answered.

She looked at his crestfallen face with pity. He seemed so young, despite his superficial air of sophistication. She felt much older than him after all she had been through in the last year. His life had been planned out for him since before he was born. She on the other hand had choices to make. She walked quickly away, stifling her tears and didn't look back.

Eliza was starting to feel more herself and the new job in Ipswich kept her busy but it had been a real struggle and she would never be the same again. She'd been let down and used but time would heal and meanwhile she had the companionship of the other servants. She was brushing the carpets in the drawing room before breakfast when Henry came in to tend to Mrs. Green's prize aspidistra. He was in charge of the indoor plants as well as the garden, and horse and carriage. She noticed how gently his strong brown hands wiped the large glossy leaves with a damp cloth. After a while, he asked her

"Do you come from Ipswich?"

"No, Blaxhall." she replied.

"We live in neighbouring villages, then, I'm from Coddenham, a few miles North East of here. My father is also a gardener. My mother and sister are called Eliza." She smiled at this and said

"Well, there's a funny thing, my father and brother are called Henry."

The bell for breakfast sounded and they quickly made their way to the kitchen for porridge, tea, bread and butter - Cook didn't like them being late for meals.

Later, at 9.15 sharp, Dr. Green and his wife gathered the staff in the main hall for prayers. Eliza felt safe when Henry was around and drew strength from his simple goodness. He was a man of her own class with the same values and she was comfortable with him. He worked just as hard outdoors as she did inside the house. Mrs. Green was particularly proud of the carriage because it gave them status and attracted a better class of patient. Few people could afford one but the doctor needed one for his work.

The four-wheeled brougham could carry two passengers and turn in a small space which was useful for house calls in town. Henry spent a lot of time feeding and grooming the horse, polishing the harness and getting him ready for riding or carriage work. As coachman, he wore a smart suit of livery when on carriage duty and lived over the coach house but took all his meals indoors in the kitchen. Cook used to complain about the smell of the stable and told him to sluice himself thoroughly at the pump before coming inside.

Henry was in a talkative mood one day at dinner, "I started as trainee under- gardener on a big estate. We had to wear a green baize apron, collar and tie, however hot it was. Orders had to be obeyed on the spot. If anyone was caught smoking they were sacked, no matter how long they had worked there. I was one of seven gardeners and if members of the family were sitting on the terrace or lawn you had to go the long way round to the compost heap, even if you were pushing a huge barrow load of weeds, to keep out of sight. In the garden, her Ladyship would suddenly appear. She used to say to us garden boys "While you're working, listen out for the family and keep out of their way if they are walking in the garden."

If she caught sight of us, she was angry and shouted "Be alert, boy! Why weren't you listening out! Swing your arms!" We were terrified of her. You had to be invisible," he said.

Eliza nodded her head in agreement, "Yes - it was the same for us maids in the house."

Henry went on "Every morning we had to put great banks of fresh flowers in the main rooms. You must never be heard or seen doing it; they just had to be there, never a dead flower or leaf; it was part of the unreal perfection of the family's lives. If you ever used your own ideas in the arrangements, the mistress would put a stop to it. It had to be done as she had ordered. When guests admired the flowers, she always took the credit herself, as if she had grown, picked and arranged them. The staff were just part of the behind-the- scenes machinery of her life - she didn't thank us.

I was taught never to speak, unless they spoke first, or even look at them. The garden was huge - seven acres. Gardening was a perfect art; there was a lot of topiary for example. That was a very responsible job - one bad clip and a pheasant became a duck."

Eliza laughed. "We made these creatures up ourselves. Sometimes we were tempted to cut out a monster that would grow and grow but of course we never did. We took a great pride in hedge cutting too. It was the hedge which set the garden off. The tops were like billiard tables." Eliza nodded admiringly.

"None of the village people were allowed into the garden. Definitely not. Trades people came to the back door but never saw the main gardens. His Lordship wouldn't let any Tom, Dick or Harry into the park, let alone the gardens."

That reminded Eliza of going into the summer house in the garden at De Vere Hall with Freddie and how nervous she had felt going into forbidden territory.

Cook said "They must have been very rich."

Henry replied "Oh, yes, they spent a lot of money on the house and garden. Lordship and Ladyship had everything they wanted, every kind of produce from the gardens, hothouses and home farm. Working there educated me and now I can talk to anybody - something we Suffolk people find hard. So I became a foreigner in the village, no longer in the village family like the rest. I belonged to the big house and it was hard to leave."

"Yes, said Eliza, "I felt the same."

"But I had a great training as a gardener and acquired all my knowledge completely free; we grew a plant from seed, potted it on, planted it and saw it growing where it would always grow - not like a nursery - growing plants to sell. I've had the fine art of tidiness drummed into me. I had to help my father in the garden when I was a boy; there was nothing else to do and it was expected of me."

Eliza asked, "Why did you leave the estate then?"

"Well, I'm young, I wanted to see something of town life, and I like working with horses as well. We used to collect the coal for heating the greenhouses from the station with a horse and cart. A horse pulled the mower too. We had to put leather shoes on the horse's hooves to stop her cutting up the ground. She was a Suffolk Punch called Bess and she used to know exactly what to do, she'd done it so often. There was too much grass for a push mower!"

"Lord De Vere used to breed Suffolk Punches - they're lovely horses."

"Yes, you know what they say about them - face of an angel, belly like a beer barrel and backside like a farmer's daughter." Eliza blushed and laughed. He went on "We lived in the garden cottage and a woman cleaned and cooked our meals. We worked from seven in the morning to five at night with an hour for lunch.

103

Saturdays we finished at 12 noon."

Eliza protested. "You had shorter working hours than we did!" Then she relented and said "But I suppose it was heavier work and you could only work in daylight."

"Yes, don't forget we were out there all weathers. It was very cold in spite of our heavy-duty trousers and boots. We needed oilskins for wet weather - we often got very wet and cold in November pruning trees. In my first year I had to wheel fallen leaves in a great heavy wheelbarrow with an iron band round the front wheel, and me and another boy used to race away, turn the load over and begin again - it was for the love of it and the pride. The vicar said to me once

"Henry it's marvellous what God can do in a garden with a gardener's help" and I told him

"Yes, but He makes a hell of a mess of it if He's left to Himself." which didn't go down too well.

Eliza laughed. Henry looked at her thoughtfully.

"It's nice to see you smile" he said. Then went on,

"My first head gardener was the old fashioned sort, with cropped whiskers, black suit and white shirt and a wooden expression that suddenly twinkled. He would either give you short shrift, or, if he had a mind, impart information and instruct us how to grow the most beautiful flowers out of the sullen ground. We always listened to him with respect.

I remember the first time I went into the house to do the flower arranging on my own. I decided to use chrysanthemums, but I'd not seen the dining room table before - it was set for eight and I'd got four vases to do and there were lots of knives and forks and glasses. The flowers had got wet as I was caught in the rain on the way up to the house. They dripped on the tablecloth. Anyway nothing was said and I got away with it."

Eliza loved listening to Henry's stories and admired his knowledge and experience with plants and in the stable. Their growing closeness added pleasure to their lives. They met in the kitchen, at prayers, on the Sunday procession to church and in the course of their duties. They saw each other every day, and their friendship slowly grew stronger. Henry loved the smell of the still room - a mixture of hot bread, coffee, lavender, pot-pourri and herbs. Eliza gave him a slice of new bread with warm jam on it. He thanked her and said

"I prefer you in that dainty black dress with the frilly apron and cap to your morning print dress."

"Thank-you, kind Sir." She bobbed him a curtsey in reply.

As time went by, she gradually felt the sadness of the last year receding. She had someone who cared for her and treated her with respect, made her feel secure. Henry would wait for her when she went out, dressed in his best, boots well-polished and a flower in his hat band. She wore her coat, hat and long skirt with black stockings. Once out of sight of the house, they linked arms and sauntered along the paths in the park together. Sometimes they went dancing, but she had to be back by nine o'clock or there would be a scolding from the mistress.

On one occasion, they were both given the afternoon off to go and see the annual parade of the

East Suffolk Militia. She and Henry watched as six hundred volunteer soldiers marched along behind the band. They wore bright scarlet tunics, with silver buttons and white belts over dark trousers with red stripes down the seams, helmets and heavy boots. Their instruments shone in the sunshine as they played a lively tune. In front was the honorary Colonel, Lord De Vere and other officers, including Freddie, on horse-back. The officer in charge shouted "Eyes right" and they all turned their heads to look at Eliza. Henry took her arm protectively as Freddie's horse shied suddenly, nearly unseating him. For her part, Eliza was glad that he had seen her with Henry.

Mrs. Green kept a close eye on the staff indoors but during the next few weeks they touched hands passing on the stairs. Soon they began to have furtive meetings in the housemaid's cupboard; Henry teased her and called her "Dorothy" which made her giggle in the darkness; fortunately, Mrs. Green's keys would jingle and warn them of her imminent arrival so they could keep quiet and not be found out They left each other notes under the back doormat and sneaked off for walks in the woods in the early hours of the morning. She met him outside in the potting shed when cook had gone out or fallen asleep after luncheon.

When she was with him, it was as if the world stood still and Eliza was speechless and bewildered by it all. She saw the world through new eyes. The stealth by which she met him made the affair all the more valued; every touch was a thrill to be remembered. She let him kiss her when they were on their own for a few minutes. Henry told her "I want to marry a girl who's been in service. They're cleaner and more thorough in their housekeeping; they can bake, clean, launder, cook and look after a man," he said.

One day he asked her to be his wife. "I earn thirteen shillings a week and get good tips from visitors when I hold their horses and stable the ones staying overnight" he added.

Eliza was overjoyed and said, "Yes - but you'll have to find another job where a cottage goes with the post. That room over the coach house isn't suitable for a married couple. And we need to save up for the furniture and things we need to set up home together." She was reluctant to let Henry make love to her as it had all gone so badly wrong for her before. But Henry persuaded her and she trusted him enough to give in to his caresses. He said it was natural for people like them to make love before marriage. In time Eliza realised she was expecting again. Although she laced herself in tight with her corset, the wedding day couldn't be put off too long, for if Mrs. Green suspected pregnancy or any bad behaviour, the result would be instant dismissal.

So the marriage plans had to be brought forward. But Henry was pleased about the baby and used to embarrass her telling her that she had good son-bearing hips. He went off to arrange the bans at their local church, St. Matthew's. He also redoubled his efforts to get another job.

Henry found a post, near his parents' home in Coddenham where he could start as soon as they were married. There was a good cottage that went with the place. Eliza bought furniture with her savings in service; she tried to copy the things in the houses where she had worked - small parlour chairs with padded backs and seats instead of the plain wooden farmhouse chairs in her parent's home. A deal table which she planned to cover with a brightly coloured cloth between meals and cooking jobs. When they handed in their joint notice Mrs. Green complained

"Eliza, you're leaving just when I've trained you up - and taking my coachman with you – It's too bad, I'm going to have such trouble finding new staff."

But the doctor wished them both well and gave Henry a hearty handshake, winking broadly at Eliza. Cook, too was sorry to see them go, for they had all got on well together.

In September, 1895, Eliza and Henry walked together to the church with her younger brother, Tom, now twenty, and the verger's wife, to be groomsman, bridesmaid and witnesses. Eliza wore her best blue dress and carried the posy of flowers Henry had picked for her. She was glowing with happiness. She couldn't have been happier if she was going to be a duchess. Afterwards they took the carrier to Coddenham and spent the day together in their new home. Henry's mother had made a special tea with a baked ham and all the family gathered round to greet them. Tom toasted them with,

> "I wish you well, I wish you joy
> And every year a girl or boy."
> Everyone laughed and said "Hear, hear".

It was a hard struggle financially. Henry painted the

cottage, planted the vegetable garden and put a pig in the sty. On the chest of drawers used as a sideboard, Eliza displayed the wedding presents from the Greens - the best tea service and a set of silver spoons. They had a few books, a shaded lamp, two wicker chairs by the hearth with cushions and antimacassars she had made herself. She added some fancy touches - a Japanese fan over a picture frame, a letter rack, curtains tied back with ribbon bows and flowers on the table.

As she set the table, she thought of the seven course dinners she'd helped to serve her employer. She remembered the big kitchens she'd worked in as she unwrapped the usual suet roly-poly pudding. Often the main meal was stew made from a pennyworth of meat, carrot and onion or she made pies and puddings, slow cooked for hours in the oven. But this was her own home and she was her own mistress now. She cooked a Sunday joint, stew once a week, but she knew that putting squares of bacon and vegetables in the black cooking pot over the fire at four o'clock as her mother had done, was the only way to eke out the thirteen shilling a week wages Henry brought in.

When her parents- in- law came to dinner and saw the flowers on the table, they laughed and said "What are we going to have, Liza, we can't eat those!" She rolled her eyes at this, she had seen more of the world and knew how things were done. It was her day now. She said,

"That's how they do things at the big house. Times are changing and marriage is more of a partnership now; as well as buying pig food and chopping wood,

Henry carries coal for me, fetches water from the well, and sweeps the path."

"That's women's work," the old folk said, shaking their heads. But Henry replied

"My Eliza works hard enough as it is, I won't have her hurt her back. I'm stronger, tis only fair to help out with the chores."

His father teased him and his mother muttered "girls are getting lazy nowadays." But Eliza noticed that her father- in- law started to help out in their house more. She herself was used to having her own money and made a bit extra keeping hens and selling eggs to the grocers.

Their first child, called Henry John, after his father and grandfather, was born a few months after the wedding. As Grandpa said,

"The lil boy turned up a bit quick; he come just in time to hev a slice of his mother's wedding cake."

The baby did much to heal Eliza's pain at the loss of her baby girl. What a contrast to the workhouse it was to have given birth to the baby at home in her own bed with Henry coming in sheepishly carrying the cup of tea the midwife had ordered, to see his new son.

He was a good husband who never kept her short of housekeeping money by spending it on drink or smoking. He was very handy in the house, and kind to her when she was ill. For her part, she schemed and provided well so that the family didn't go without. She never complained and kept the place spotless. To her great joy, they had a daughter next. Eliza called her Hilda Rose, after her own little sister. It was lovely to have a baby girl she could love and keep; watch her grow up and hear her calling her Mother.

Whenever she could, she did odd jobs to help with the finances. She felt a warm glow every time she looked up and saw Henry coming home to their little cottage. In the evenings, they would sit by the fire while she mended or made clothes for the children as her mother had taught her all those years ago. The fire was the heart of the home; the flickering flames, the crackle of burning logs and the warmth had a calming effect on them, cementing the bond between them.

Henry John wore dresses until he was breeched at three years old. She had to cut down his clothes to make them fit Hilda Rose. When she'd put them to bed upstairs, Henry would take up the newspaper and read bits of it out to her that he thought would interest her. They would talk about the children, who were their pride and joy and made their happiness complete.

The children didn't know where babies came from and there were no books about childbirth. Eliza always wore a long coat outside if she was expecting, even in the hot weather.

"Dad, why is Mum getting so fat?" asked little Henry John at the table one day. Eliza spluttered into her tea cup.

"She's been eating too many dumplings" laughed Henry.

Eliza told the children that babies came from the cabbage patch. Their second little boy was born in 1899 and they called him Frederick William. Eliza remembered those were Baron De Vere's names. Her mother had written that his Lordship was giving Bertha a generous allowance. She could never talk to

Henry about this though, as it must be kept quiet.

She was often tired and discouraged by all the hard work. Sometimes she looked back to her years in service as good times. But soon the older children would be able to help out more, she thought. The furnishings they had bought second hand - the clock and a looking glass, gave her much satisfaction and she kept them spotless. When the housework was done, she would look round at the rooms with their engravings and feel a sense of pride in her home.

She reflected on her mother saying "You'll be a housewife and mother when you grow up – same as me, same as your grandmother."

She remembered her childish dreams of being a teacher, bettering herself, but now she was Henry's wife and had three lovely children, life wasn't so bad after all. While she had a strip wash with carbolic soap from a bowl on the kitchen table and water from the cold tap in the yard, she thought of Freddie and their hopes of marriage. Foolish dreams of youth which could never have come true. This was the life she was suited for. As the children cleaned their teeth with brushes dipped in a tin of tooth powder and went to the toilet in the privy at the end of the garden, she constantly thought of little Bertha growing up without her. But at least, she would have the chance of a better life with the De Vere family.

When it got dark, Eliza lit candles and the paraffin lamp. She had swept out the coal fire in the morning. Now she placed cinders in the bottom of the grate, paper and a few thin sticks of wood covered sparsely with coal to allow air to kindle the flames. Just as her relationship with Henry was built slowly, she thought, with care and kindness, not like her passion for Freddie which had flared up like a paper fire, burned brightly for a short time and soon turned to ashes. She lit the fire as it was really cold. Her love for Henry had grown out of friendship and would burn for a long time. She added larger pieces of coal. They would add more love gently as time went by, to keep the flame alive.

Next morning she hung the mats on the line and beat them. She had turned the sheets sides to middle and patched them. When she was hanging out the washing and working outside the neighbours often came out for a chat. Eliza knew they judged her on the whiteness of her laundry and her skilful housework gave her the respectability she craved after her disreputable past. It was a good chance to have a gossip.

"A woman's work is never done" the woman next door called out to her. Then when sheets, pillow cases and towels were billowing in the wind on the line the whole length of the garden Eliza invited her "Come in and have a cup of tea."

"Well you've got a nice place here," the neighbour said.

"Yes that lace table cloth belonged to my old granny," said Eliza, "and that chair's been in the family for years." She viewed the neat piles of snowy linen on the lined closet shelves with pleasure. Nice and clean and fresh, she thought, breathing in the scent of lavender and country air.

"Cleanliness is next to godliness" her neighbour

commented. "Where did you work before you was married, Eliza?" she asked.

Eliza told her little and hoped she wouldn't ask too many questions.

She valued her neighbours' friendship. She needed their acceptance so kept her past a secret and the front doorstep spotless. The neighbours stood at their doors with their arms folded chatting away noticing everything she did and commenting on it.

She recalled her mother's sharp voice when she was a child at home. How irritable she always was with her! Now she understood better how her mother felt, especially with ten children to look after. At least she only had three. She tried to be as patient and loving with Hilda as she was with the boys, bearing in mind how much her mother's favouritism of the boys had hurt her in the past.

She looked at her hands sadly - they were red and sore now from washing up heavy pans of iron and copper in hot soda water in the shallow stone sink; rubbing the iron spoons and forks with brick dust; boiling the table cloths and pillow cases in starch powder. Not fit to wear Freddie's ring now even if she wanted to. The papers were full of advertisements proclaiming "Get rid of Dirt and Disease – Use Bleach!" or Caustic Soda or Carbolic Acid. She knew germs lurked everywhere, invisible, causing sickness and death. She had scrubbed in the workhouse to cleanse her sins, and now she did it to protect her family. She would do anything to keep them safe. Die for them if necessary.

In the evening, while she was mending woollen

socks and stockings and patching clothes, Henry mended the shoes and boots by cutting out leather pieces and fitting new soles and heels. Every now and then they would look over at each other and smile in companionable silence.

Eliza had to shop every day, because there was only a cupboard to store food. Often she could only afford a pennyworth of anything anyway. The shop smelt glorious; fresh bread, roasted coffee beans, tea in mysterious boxes from India, fresh farm butter, coarse dark sugar, spices and dried fruits. Eliza breathed it all in; even though she could not afford many of the goods, she could still enjoy the smell. The broken biscuits were cheap - everything was weighed for her, nothing was in packets, just big sacks for the shop keeper to scoop out and put it on the scales.

Before pay day, she often ran short of money and had to ask for "trust" from the shop. This was entered into a little book and had to be paid off at the end of the week before she could buy anything else. If they desperately needed money, she sometimes took a bundle of clothing or other belongings to the pawn shop where it was exchanged for cash plus an extra 3d to get it back.

She had to manage the budget carefully and count every penny; every week she paid into a clothing club for clothes and shoes for the children. It was a hard life but they had each other and were very happy. But she still found her thoughts drifting to Bertha and wondered how she was getting on.

Chapter Seven - Bertha at the Hall

Bertha grew up the apple of the family's eye, years younger than the rest of the family - she was very much the baby. Her eldest brother, Jack, a merchant seaman, and when he was at home on leave he would take her onto his lap and cuddle her. Her older sisters, Rose and Maud fussed over her, helping her dress, and playing with her. Maud had progressed from pupil to monitor at the village school and then to pupil-teacher. She hoped to emerge eventually as a fully-fledged teacher. So it was a crushing disappointment when the headmistress heard about Eliza's disgrace from their nosy neighbour, who was jealous of the attention the family was getting from Miss Cecelia de Vere. The head mistress therefore dismissed Maud from her position as pupil teacher. She told her "We can't have any immorality in this school, your family is not respectable."

So both the girls had to go into service a few years later.

Cecilia continued to make regular visits to the cottage; Bertha had charmed her as a newborn baby in a little white cap. A spinster, keeping house for her father, she knew nothing much of babies and had a sentimental vision of Bertha growing into an angelic little girl, playing in the garden and listening to bedtime stories. But she must watch over this child - it was her Christian duty – and it was unthinkable that her brother's daughter should become a mere village girl. Her future must be very different.

On Bertha's fourth birthday, she gave her a book of

bible stories with pictures to look at. Now that the child was older, Cecelia decided it was time to invite her to tea at the Hall; she could order a pink iced cake. She grieved to see that the child had picked up a broad Suffolk accent and dialect words of the labouring classes and wanted to correct these and be a good influence on her. At the Hall, the child would be in the care of a carefully chosen nurse for a while at least. She smiled, thinking of herself as Pharaoh's daughter finding baby Moses in the bulrushes and letting a Hebrew woman to look after him until the child was old enough to come to the Egyptian court. Proper speech was of the utmost importance. She would speak to Papa right away.

The next day, in his study at the Hall, Lord de Vere had come to a decision.

"The child is part of the family - in a way."

His agent disagreed, "She's simply an unfortunate…. wrong side of the blanket. Happens all the time. They can't prove that it's Frederick's child anyway."

"But she is in fact a de Vere, you do realise that."

The agent nodded silently, then amended, "Only partly, my Lord."

"She's my grandchild. In my book that makes her a de Vere." The Baron was getting angry now.

"Perhaps" said the agent it would be better not to know anything about it. The child can't take her father's name, or inherit his money. She has no legal rights."

"Ignorance is bliss, you mean?" The Baron drew himself up to his full height. "That is not the way I think. I have already agreed to pay maintenance for the child - that assumes some sort of responsibility. I couldn't allow Frederick's daughter to be brought up in poverty. What sort of a life would she have? We must look after her, educate her.

"But to have her here" the agent was shocked.... "The gossip... And aren't you forgetting something - the other grandparents? They may not wish her to come."

"I shall send an invitation through Cecilia, she visits there regularly," replied the Baron in a tone which settled the matter once and for all.

So one sunny morning in April, as the trees were softened with fresh green, Miss Cecilia came to the cottage at Pump Square and graciously issued an invitation, on her father's behalf, to Sarah to bring the child up to the Hall the following Sunday afternoon.

When she had gone, Jack exploded, "Very kind of her, I'm sure."

"Jack, use your head - we need them, said Sarah, "if we want the best for Bertha - what's rightfully hers - she should go up to the Hall. I don't want her to go without - they can help her to a better life than we can. We can't afford to be proud, Son. Miss de Vere didn't mean any harm. She thinks of us as the lower orders. She's right - we are a different class to her. But Bertha's grandfather has the right to see her too."

"Well, I'm not touching my forelock to 'em." said Jack, "That's why I chose to go to sea in the merchant navy - no man looks down on me there."

On Sunday afternoon, a pony carriage duly pulled up outside the cottage and Sarah and Bertha, who was waiting eagerly at the window, came out and the driver handed them into it. They set off, the pony's bridle jingling, the carriage rocking over the bumpy road to de Vere village, a few miles away. As they neared their destination, the carriage followed a mile of high stone wall and finally swept through the lodge gates. The lodge house was built in an intricate gothic style. The lodge keeper came out to close the gates behind them and stared curiously as they went by.

Sarah tried to keep Bertha sitting still beside her as they travelled. But she kept jumping up and trying to lean out. She was dressed in her best clothes - her dark hair brushed and shining.

"Now remember your manners when you meet his Lordship."

It was a daunting prospect to meet this great man face to face. He was a legend in the district, a friend of the Prince of Wales.

Sarah gasped with amazement as the magnificent house appeared in the distance. As the mansion loomed bigger and bigger, she felt smaller and smaller. The carriage continued up the drive and came to a halt beneath the stone portico at the front door. They climbed down, helped by the driver. He rang the doorbell for them. A black coated butler opened the huge door and bowed as they stepped hesitantly inside. The hall floor was laid with blue, yellow and white tiles. The carpet and curtains were crimson, the walls and pillars were marble. Sarah was shocked to see the white sculpture of a reclining nude standing out in stark contrast against the rich colours. There were paintings of racehorses on the walls.

The butler announced them at the door of the drawing room. It was a pretty space, with big windows, flower arrangements, gilded mirrors, and chandeliers. The Baron's three daughters, all in their late twenties, were sitting bolt upright. Cecelia smiled encouragingly at Bertha. Lord de Vere himself rose to greet them - he was a benign -looking man with an olive complexion, dark hair, big black beard. His eyes twinkled behind a lorgnette. Impeccably dressed in dark coat, grey trousers and white stock, he spoke kindly and welcomed them into the room.

"So this is the little girl is it?" He studied her intently, as though looking for family resemblances.

"About time we had some young ones about the house again." The ladies looked down at their laps at this. "Come in and have some tea, won't you."

Bertha's jaw dropped. Her eyes took in currant buns, cucumber sandwiches, chocolate biscuits and best of all, a pink-iced cake. They sat down and Bertha chose a slice of pink cake, declined a cucumber sandwich and ate a selection of everything else. Sarah hoped she wouldn't be sick.

"Good appetite, I'm glad to see," the Baron nodded approvingly.

After half an hour of stilted conversation about the weather and Bertha' health, the baron rang for the maid and told her to show them to the gardens at the back of the house,

"Let the little girl play for a while before leaving - please come and visit us again, my dear," he said, in parting.

Sarah and Bertha went outside on to the terrace at

the back of the house. Beyond the stone balustrades, they could see formal flower beds laid out below them. Elegant stone greyhounds flanked the steps. Bertha rushed down and along a winding path to where a large tree stood with a swing hanging from its gnarled branches. She called out to Sarah to hoist her up and then called out

"Push me, push me, higher, higher!" as she lay back on the wooden seat, she kicked up her legs, laughing at the flying sensation and the relief of getting away from the stiff atmosphere in the drawing room and all the grownups' questions about what she liked doing.

She could see strange trees; a big clump of grass with creamy plumes waving in the breeze, an ornamental pond with a dolphin fountain splashed in the middle. Suddenly, she jumped off the swing and ran to the pond to see if there were any fish, but when she saw how big they were she drew back in fear, and started to run round the stone path instead. Sarah called out,

"Be careful, or you'll fall in."

They spent a happy hour there before Sarah said "I think we'd better go now."

"No, I don't want to" protested Bertha, "this is the best place I've ever been - I want to stay here forever!"

"Come along now" coaxed Sarah, "It's time to go home. You can come again and visit - but not if you're naughty."

They went home in the carriage to Pump Square - Bertha's eyes sparkling with all the things she had seen that day, to tell Father and her older brothers and sisters

"It was wonderful up at the big house and I met the Lord and the ladies and had a drink of lemonade and lots of lovely things to eat…".while they looked on indulgently and were pleased for her.

Their neighbours - the shepherd, the cow man, the farm workers, were amazed at first when they saw the carriage drive up outside the little cottage and wondered where they were going. Agnes, the woman next door, was a bit sour of course. There was plenty of talk about it at first, but then as time went on, the neighbours accepted it and went about their business - there was plenty of work to do and they had their own lives to lead.

Bertha, herself, as many children have to, learned to live in the two worlds of cottage and Hall, gradually learning to switch between them. She was young and able to adapt to the rules and habits of each. When Miss Cecilia visited her at home, she had to stand up straight and answer questions about how she was getting on. She brought her expensive presents. One day, she presented Bertha with a beautifully dressed porcelain doll. And on Bertha's next visit to the Hall, she was joined by a little boy, a playmate a year younger than herself. This was Lawrence, son of Adeline, the eldest married sister, who had come to stay for a visit. His Nanny took the children out in the morning and afternoon for a walk, put them down for a rest after dinner at one o'clock and brought them down to the drawing room before tea to be left with the family for twenty minutes or so. She coached Bertha into speaking properly but the girl would lapse into the Suffolk dialect when she was at home or with the other villagers.

Nurse kept a watchful eye on the two children as they played in the garden; there were broad steps between delphinium spikes, an avenue of shady trees, a grass covered court, a sundial and flowers. Bertha was happy. Everyone spoke kindly to her with soft agreeable voices. Cecelia showed her an aviary,

"What pretty coloured birds!" exclaimed Bertha, "What are they called?"

"There are too many to give them names," laughed Cecelia.

All the people were beautiful, dressed in lovely clothes. They took her into a spacious cool palace, full of splendid things. There was a gallery of pictures, wonderful games.

Outside again, the groom brought round a donkey from the stables and placed Lawrence carefully into a side basket. Best of all, he brought out a little black pony out for Bertha. She was thrilled and threw her arms round the pony's neck at once, crying

"Is he mine, is he really mine? I'll call him Blackie."

The groom said, "I'll teach you to ride him."

He helped her to mount, then led them round the park. From then on, she hardly thought, spoke, or dreamt of anything else but her pony and riding. She watched the groom brushing her pony; whistling and murmuring, "Now then, little lad."

She loved the stables; the smell of leather, horses and hay. She adored Blackie's velvet muzzle, shaggy neck and big dark eyes. When she left, the ladies called out to her "Come back soon!"

At School

Bertha started going to the village school when she was five and walked the two miles each way. Attendance at school was now both compulsory and free. If it was raining the children had to sit in damp clothes. For lunch they brought bread and dripping or jam. Bertha noticed that some of the other children had dirty, torn clothes and some had no shoes. Her dress and pinafore were the cleanest, she thought to herself. She had no younger brothers or sisters to care for at home, but she still had to help Mother with the chores.

There were sixty children at school, sitting in one long room, divided into groups managed by the head mistress, assistant teacher and one pupil teacher – the room smelt of boots, the coke stove, chalk and ink. The lowest class was called "The Babies" and many of the infants were barely out of the crawling stage. Katie, who lived next door to Bertha at Pump Square, was three. Her mother was ill and had another baby to look after, so the schoolmistress agreed to take Katie. On the first day, she sat on a stool by the fire - she had a red petticoat and the children called her `Little Polly Flinders - sitting in the cinders` and laughed at her.

Bertha herself had to endure some taunts and name calling from other children and one, a freckled faced girl with a turned up nose, reminded her she was in the world on sufferance - "My mother says that children like you should never have been born!"

Bertha retaliated,

"I'm going to tell my Mother and Father of you!"

But the girl spat back,

"That's not your mother, and he's not your father either!"

Bertha ran home to her mother in tears and Sarah wrapped her arms around her and told her it was all nonsense.

"She's just trying to make trouble - I'll have a word with her mother."

Bertha held her head up high and reminded herself that only she was invited up to the big house. She had every right to be here. She was as good as anyone, in fact, she was better.

By now the children she played with at the Hall included the three children of Marianne, the Baron's youngest daughter, who were younger than herself, who often came to visit.

Sometimes when it was raining, the children at the Hall went upstairs to the long gallery used as a playroom and got the dressing up clothes out of the chest. They play-acted and rode on the rocking horse. Aunt Cecilia told them about the portraits that hung there; "Look, these are your ancestors"

There was one of an eighteenth century French aristocratic lady in a blue silk embroidered gown with lace, her hair powdered.

"She looks like you, Bertha."

Bertha put on a long dress, piled her long hair up and cavorted in front of the mirror, thinking, "One day I'll be a great lady - you'll see!"

The village children spent all day at school chanting tables, weights and measures. The boys played at one end of the playground, the girls at the other. They learned to make cubes, pyramids and cylinders in the great iron-framed desks. They used simple readers and slates and chalk for writing. The teacher insisted the children sat still in silence and expected complete obedience. If Bertha made a mistake the teacher instantly punished her with a rap on the knuckles with her ruler. Many of the children, especially the boys, didn't attend often as they had to work in the fields; the farmer used to keep the boys away for weeding the fields, even though that was now breaking the law. Their parents needed the wages.

Fortunately, Bertha didn't have to work in the fields as her older siblings had done because Sarah received money from the Hall and Cecelia didn't want her to do heavy work, or get sunburnt. Sometimes she would see other school children picking potatoes in the field, lugging heavy baskets and bending down all day. The farm work was poorly paid and Bertha's brothers decided to answer an advert in the paper seeking farm workers in Yorkshire.

Mother didn't want them to go and was sad when Arthur and Tom went away, soon to be followed by Maud, who had found work as a domestic servant in London. At least London was an adventure and might offer her some better opportunities and the chance to get on. And, as Father said philosophically, it was fewer mouths to feed.

About this time they had some good news; Jack, Bertha's merchant seaman brother, had been away for months and they feared his ship was sunk and he had drowned. One night, there was a knocking at the cottage door and when father went down to open it - there was the sailor `home from the sea`. When they all gathered round to ask him why he had taken so long to get home, he replied with a twinkle in his blue eyes, "Well, the ship did go down, but we were rescued. Then we arrived in Liverpool but my pay ran out and I had to walk all the way home doing odd jobs on the way!"

"You could've written, Tom" said mother. "We were so worried."

"Didn't have the time or money for letters, Mother," he replied cheerfully.

Agricultural labourers were poor, crops didn't bring in much money and even farmers were hanging on with difficulty. Preservation of game birds on Lord De Vere's estate was a top priority at this time and there was a small army of keepers dressed in a livery of blue velvet with buttons bearing their master's coat of arms parading about the countryside. Many of the better workers had left the land to emigrate or find work elsewhere in Britain.

The villagers were pleased the children were getting an education, but it did nothing for the family budget in the short term. Sarah didn't need Parish relief but most agricultural workers couldn't bring up their families without it. Sometimes men were so hungry they stole turnips out of the field for food. But still farm workers continued to be given small wages, laid off at slack times and sent home without pay in wet weather. Some men despaired and committed suicide. The brook was deep enough to drown in. Bertha pitied the old men with hunched backs- some almost bent double from working out in the fields in all weathers and hardly able to walk. When they finally retired, they got eighteen pence a week and a small loaf of bread, and lived in terror of being sent to the workhouse.

To help the men, Lord De Vere kindly gave some land for allotments. A quarter of an acre each plot at £1.12s.0d annual rent. The villagers were grateful and grew mainly potatoes, vegetables, corn for their hens and for baking; the Stones' neighbour had a small plough and donkey; he harnessed his sow with the donkey when it refused to pull alone. Later he acquired a pony which he hired out to other allotments. They used unwanted farm implements and stored them in their makeshift sheds. The Baron was also pleased, he told his friends

"These allotments keep families from applying for Poor Relief, poaching and stealing."

However, Bertha's father commented drily that his Lordship was charging villagers rent for land landowners had taken from them at the time of the Enclosures. But he took an allotment all the same. After it had been ploughed, Bertha followed where her father's dibber made holes four inches apart, dropping grains - four in each hole. He taught her the old Suffolk rhyme;

> Four seeds in a hole;
> One for the rook, one for the crow,
> One to rot and one to grow.

Bertha also enjoyed the singing lessons at school. They learnt songs like "Make hay while the sun shines" and "Will you sign the Pledge?" Many children signed up that they would never take a drop of alcohol in their life. Bertha didn't – she saw how father enjoyed his pint of beer. She was good at needlework, sums and English. She loved the class celebrations of Empire Day every year on Queen Victoria's birthday, 24th May. Then, on the Queen's Diamond Jubilee when Bertha was six, the children decorated the classroom with union jack flags and had lessons on the "Growth and Extent of the British Empire." The world map was mostly coloured pink to show the empire on which the sun never set. Teacher told them,

"Britain leads the world in trade, finance and shipping, and, with our manufacturing and mining industries, London is the financial centre of the world. Wealth flows in from our Empire." But it hasn't reached our village yet, thought Bertha, as they launched into "Rule Britannia" feeling very proud and patriotic.

The girls had been practicing a tableau especially for the occasion. They went out of the classroom to get ready and came back draped in flags and pieces of muslin to represent the countries in the Empire. Silence fell as the girls each announced themselves and took their place in the tableau.

"I am India," said Bertha, pulling some muslin across her face to make a veil, "the jewel in the crown." She had taken off her high buttoned boots and combed her dark chestnut hair and Ernest in the front row thought she looked beautiful. Then the children all sang "Rule Britannia" again. After lunch the teachers organised games.

Next day the teacher told the children:

"The greatest progress in the education of the British people has been made in the last fifty years." But she added with a sniff, "Education is still very substandard, especially in this school."

Sometimes she caned the older boys in front of the class, and Bertha really hated it when this happened. She didn't like to see others suffer. Many of the children didn't care much about book learning - as long as they could learn enough to measure a shed, read a swine disease warning or write out a bill, no more was needed. They knew they were going to follow in their mothers' and fathers' footsteps, but Bertha worked hard at her lessons, she knew she was destined for something better.

Cecelia visited the school one day to Bertha's delight and gave prizes of sweets and pocket handkerchiefs. She praised the children's singing of "You can't Play in Our Yard" and Bertha glowed with pride.

One morning in 1898 when Bertha was seven, and Eliza was visiting her parents, there was great excitement all over the district. The jangling bells of St. Mary's church and a messenger summoned the fire brigade to a fire at De Vere Hall. Eliza and Bertha joined the other villagers hurrying to the scene. The word was that it had started in a chimney flue in the kitchen. Soon after, it spread to the north wing. It was some time before the arrival of the fire brigade, as the men had to harness the horses up to the cart. Servants and villagers worked hard to check the flames but soon the fire was blazing furiously. Gamekeepers and stablemen removed furniture and other contents, including valuable paintings, from the building.

Eliza was afraid - the night came back to her vividly, when she had been on her way to the workhouse and had passed by De Vere Hall. She'd stumbled on the rough grass and instinctively put her hand across her belly to protect her unborn child. As she pulled her shawl tighter around her shoulders she had turned to look back at the Hall, now gleaming white in the moonlight where she'd been seduced and betrayed. Her words came back to her now like a fearful judgment upon her.

"Curse you all! And may this house fall stone by stone for what you've done to me."

Then she'd set off again for Wickham Market and the Workhouse. She hadn't looked back any more, sunk in her own thoughts; a baby I can't keep, a love turned sour, and broken dreams of a better life I can never have.

Now she had her revenge. She stood in the crowd watching as pieces of fine furniture were lowered by rope from the upper windows and lighter articles thrown out on to the lawn. The police were there and guarded the accumulated pile. Water had to be pumped from the lake at the rear of the house. The wind picked up and fanned the orange flames into fury. The crown stepped back from the heat. The upper rooms looked like raging furnaces. Windows cracked and shattered, lead poured from the gables in molten streams, while vertical cracks appeared in several places in the façade, warning everyone to keep their distance. The fine turret remained intact for five hours but, within minutes of being attacked, the spire with weather vane and the heavy brass bell fell to the ground with a loud crash. The roof was of pitch pine and burnt like tinder, helping the fire to spread to every part of the mansion surprisingly quickly.

By noon, five fire engines had reached the scene. Although the men worked tirelessly, nothing could stop the relentless destruction amid the noise of floors crashing down, the cracking of plate glass and the hubbub of voices from the spectators gathered from far and near. Vehicles and cyclists kept arriving to see the disaster. Eliza called out

"Is the family trapped inside?"

Someone answered "No, no-one's at home to day."

Eliza was relieved. Lord De Vere was summoned from London and arrived by the midday train with the rest of his family. Eliza's heart was in her mouth again, as she saw Freddie running into the burning Hall to bring out the family's treasured possessions.

She saw figures moving about inside the library, then there was a great crash and part of the ceiling fell in. Freddie appeared at the open window with a bloody gash on his forehead. He hesitated for a moment. Then he leapt out on to the lawn where he fell and lay still. Eliza pressed through the crowd with Bertha to see if he was alright. A doctor arrived and examined him. She heard him say,

"You'll recover, young man, but that was a foolish thing to do - you could have broken your neck."

She realized the anger she'd once felt towards him had now melted away. But the fire continued to burn into the evening and it was late when she, Bertha and the last onlookers finally drifted away.

The destruction of the old Hall was a dreadful blow to the De Vere family. They had to move into the Dower House much shaken. It took two years to rebuild the Hall with the insurance money but this could never completely replace their loss.

Three years later, in 1901, there was more sadness when the old Queen died aged 82. The village shops put up their shutters and all the men wore black armbands. The church bell tolled all day - teacher cried but Ernest said "The good old gal will get the best seat in heaven, so why be sad?"

And the children had to agree. The workers were given a day off for her funeral. After going to church, they all went to the pub to drink to her memory and the new King's health.

The coronation of King Edward VII was an occasion for national rejoicing and therefore was scheduled for 26th June 1902 when the newspapers said the end of the Boer War was assured and victory in sight. However, the King's doctors advised him that he needed an operation to remove his appendix. The Coronation must be postponed!

The villagers had collected a lot of money for the food and drink. This had already been delivered when the news of the postponement arrived. So, as a compromise, everyone went to the church to pray for the King's recovery before the celebrations went ahead as planned. After the feast there were sports for the children while the grownups had a nap. At tea everyone got tickets for the roundabouts and swing boats and free issues of beer and ginger pop. Bertha's father was very interested in the huge new traction engine which drove a dynamo providing electric light as dusk fell. "Good bye Dolly I must leave you" blared out of the fairground organ and she saw courting couples wandering off into the darkness looking for a quiet spot.

The day ended with a speech wishing the king a quick return to health and certainly plenty of people had drunk to it! They all went home tired and happy and on 9th August, a slimmer and more relaxed King was crowned. Bertha saw the Baron at the Hall dressed in his coronation robes of red velvet, with white ermine cape and silver gilt coronet. She and the other grandchildren admired him and listened as he told them what would happen at the Abbey.

"All the peers will swear allegiance to the King, kneel before him, touch the crown upon his head and kiss his right hand. Then the drums will beat and the trumpets sound and all the people will shout God save the king!"

And Bertha never forgot the wonderful day she dressed in a beautiful white dress with a big flower-garlanded hat and was taken to De Vere Hall by Cecilia to watch the King arrive for a visit with Lord De Vere in his fine coach and horses. She'd been practising her curtsey for weeks. The gentlemen bowed and doffed their hats to the ladies but she was disappointed that the King wasn't wearing the golden crown and red velvet robes like the picture in her school classroom. Still, she felt honoured and privileged to be there.

More excitement was to come. When Bertha was

twelve, Cecilia allowed her to join the hunt. She gave her a riding habit, crop and gloves and she looked a picture, sitting side-saddle on her immaculately groomed hunter, her chestnut hair swept up into a bun and a black bowler hat crammed on top. The season started in August. Breakfast was served at 6am and they had to be out on their horses by half past.

The Master and hunt servants wore red coats and velvet hats as they all gathered on the lawn of De Vere Hall. The butler wove around the horses, carrying stirrup cups on a silver tray. Lord De Vere no longer hunted, he preferred shooting, but he surveyed the hounds and horse riders benevolently from the front steps of the rebuilt mansion, making a short speech to send them on their way

"Good luck, Ladies and gentlemen. It does your liver good - a good run across country. I've faced many a fence and taken many a tumble in my day."

Then they were off! The difficult fences and rough country took stamina and courage and added enjoyment and a sense of purpose to Bertha's daily life in the country during the dull days of winter. It was thrilling, with the sound of the horn and the barking of the hounds and there was a sense of achievement after a hard day. Bertha wrote in her diary that evening; "Found in covert behind the house. Soon lost fox but picked up another and ran with it very fast to the turf near the beach, where the hunt looked a fine sight. A wonderful day - hours in the saddle and we went ten miles." She was staying at the Hall overnight and went out to the stables. Lights shone out where the grooms were brushing down the horses. She said

"Give her some more oats, Potts, so she beats the others at the Hunt tomorrow."

"Alright, Miss Bertha," he replied "but be careful, you'll hurt yourself one of these days."

Bertha took no notice. Next morning, riding her chestnut mare, who had succeeded Blackie, she navigated the tricky fences and banks and thought it was glorious sport. She loved tearing across the countryside in the thrill of the chase. The crowning moment of glory was when the huntsman presented her with the fox's brush at her first kill.

She arrived back dirty and dishevelled at the Hall and the footman had to help her off with her muddy boots. She trailed upstairs to get changed out of her riding things and have a bath. Then it was time to go home again, to her elderly parents in Pump Square. They were now in their sixties and suffering aches and pains, although they still worked as hard as ever. They puzzled over her. Sarah said

"I don't know why she wants to go gallivanting over the country on a horse, chasing foxes – we never did."

"Well I suppose it's in her blood" said her father "she gets it from them. They're giving her special privileges. I hope it means a good future for her, not the drudgery we had – it's her birthright after all."

Meanwhile Bertha had to come down to earth with a bump. The next day was a school day and she met up with her friends Helen, who was a shepherd's daughter, and Lovethine who was from the gypsy encampment on the Common. Some of the other girls resented Bertha as she grew up and said she "put on airs and graces". When she walked across the playground, she heard laughter and turned to find that freckled faced girl mincing behind her with her nose in the air. Bertha flew at her and tore her hair ribbon out, but just then the bell went and they all had to line up to file in.

"Don't worry about her" whispered Lovethine at break – "I'll put a gypsy curse on her, that'll fix her. You can't help what you are, Bertha, you're not like the rest of us. Someday you'll go far away from here and have a different life from this."

Lovethine took Bertha home to meet her family, who were hawkers and poachers; they camped on the common in tents and caravans and hunted with their greyhounds. Her mother made wooden pegs, little boxes of sallow wood decorated with shells and lace, and made up other small items such as packets of pins, hooks and eyes to sell out of her large wicker basket.

Lovethine showed Bertha where there was a fox burrow in the wood. They went out early and hid to watch a vixen emerge with her cubs, who played with an old rabbit skin while she squatted on her haunches, ears quivering as she listened for danger. The girls kept upwind of her. Once, she gave a short low bark and she and all the cubs froze as an old badger went grunting along in search of his breakfast.

When the cubs were tired of play, the vixen would take them back to the burrow, then reappear and trot off, returning soon with a rabbit in her jaws. Later, she brought them out and washed them with her tongue. The dog fox came along with dinner. They both sniffed over what he had brought. Then he stretched out beside her and nuzzled her with his tongue behind the ears till distant sounds made him pick up the dinner and lead his family back to the burrow. On the way back to the caravan, Lovethine said

"How could you kill such lovely creatures at the hunt, Bertha?"

"Well, they kill our chickens, don't they?" she replied.

There was a village legend that, when the Black Death of 1348 had killed off all the villagers, gypsies had moved in, settled down and were never wholly displaced. Certainly there were some fair people in the village and some very dark handsome ones with blue black hair.

Bertha was heartbroken when the gypsies were turned off the common because their horses and donkeys were getting into the allotments and being put to graze in the farmers' fields at night, then being retrieved before daylight. The Parish Council banished them and a body of men marched from the Ship Inn in a column headed by men playing the trumpet and mouth organ. They met with no resistance for the gypsies had had word and the horses and ponies were harnessed ready to pull the caravans up to the road. The police were waiting on the high road to force them to move to another parish. Bertha waved until they were out of sight, "I'll never fergit you!" Lovethine called.

"Good luck!" shouted back Bertha, "I'll miss you – you were my best friend."

Chapter Eight - Moving on

There was great excitement at the Hall because Cecilia's younger sister, Miriam, was getting married at the late age of thirty six. But, as Nanny said to Bertha, now aged twelve:

"She had to go for the nursery for him - he's ten years younger than her - same age as Percy." The old lady smiled proudly.

Bertha was interested,

"Can I come to the wedding?"

"Oh, no, dear – that wouldn't do at all. You're too young to go about in society."

But Bertha felt like Cinderella - she never got to go to the ball. She was never invited out with the family, even to children's parties. She had been told it would cause embarrassment and might prove inconvenient to their hosts. She could never be fully accepted as a respectable De Vere.

But she still admired her aunt's clothes and the tales of the fabulous life she led in London and county society. She often crept upstairs to open her aunt's wardrobe and gaze at the chiffon and lace dresses. She reached out to touch the enormous picture hats for Ascot, cotton and linen outfits for yachting, white muslin with silk sashes for tea on the lawn and tea gowns for an afternoon in the boudoir. She stroked the fur trimmed velvet coat and smelt the bunch of Parma violets pinned on; pulled open a drawer of pink crepe de chine underwear trimmed with cream lace. She fingered the silks and breathed in the perfume, just as Eliza, her mother, had done long ago.

She caught glimpses of the Baron and Frederick looking just as elegant; black morning coats with beautifully fitting dark blue or black overalls strapped down over polished black boots and blunt silver spurs for riding; tweed knickerbocker suits for shooting, often with Tyrolean style hats made popular by the King, or white tie and tails for dinner parties. She found Lord De Vere a rather remote figure; loving but distant, a majestic being with all-seeing knowledge, an Olympian.

Still, life held some pleasures for her too and she would run outside to stroke the horses and talk to the stablemen in the stud who were discussing the breeding programme;

"The broodmare is very important if you want good stock, Miss Bertha," Potts said, with a wise nod of his head. She knew that there was something wrong with her breeding; she heard the servants whispering about her sometimes. She felt as out of place here as she did at school. She felt sad about it and wondered if there was anywhere she would fit in. She had many questions in her mind which she wasn't supposed to ask.

"That's not for young ears," the servants would say.

Still she enjoyed the excitement when there were parties at the Hall for the races, shooting, hunting, tennis and croquet, Christmas and Easter, high days and holidays, filling the house with chatter and laughter; the house smelt delicious, a combination of scented flowers from the hothouses, fragrant oils in burners and pot pourri. Then Bertha would help select the grapes and pineapples from the greenhouse and watch the gardener pick the peaches and nectarines growing on the south wall. She looked hungrily at the food being prepared in the kitchen.

"Don't touch, Miss Bertha!" said Cook, "I've arranged those canapes perfectly, ready to go upstairs. Have one of these that didn't turn out right – I'm keeping them for staff supper tonight."

A horse fair was held every Easter Monday in Woodbridge, a pretty old town on the coast, a few miles away and Bertha was taken there to see Lord De Vere's Suffolk Punch horses entered for the Show on the Fen Meadow. These farm horses with their beautiful chestnut coats and rounded lines were popular because of their hardy build, their short legs and barrel bodies - like Mr. Punch.

Horse dealers from all over Suffolk attended; the streets were full of country folk and majestic Suffolk Punches coming from the station. Bertha gazed in wonder as they shied and sidled in glossy magnificence through the crowds. They showed their paces as they were being led up and down the main high street. This was the chief breed to be sold; one of the Punch's outstanding qualities was its pulling power, which made it very attractive to City merchants, who wanted a reliable draught horse to pull their heavy wagons from the docks to their warehouses, so crowds of London horse dealers also attended the fair, looking for horses that would get down on their knees in their efforts to move a fallen tree. They checked to see if they could also back up with a cart, essential in town.

The groom told Bertha, as she fondled a horse's

ears.

"Ah, these horses are the best workers, determined, long working life, quickness in starting and can go hours without feeding."

"Good boy," said Bertha, patting the horse's strong neck.

The stallions on the showground steamed and snorted in their hessian cubicles as mere dwarfs of men rubbed them down and plaited their fair manes.

Every entrance and space in the town was filled with stalls selling brandy snaps, sweets and nuts. Bertha couldn't resist the smell and bought some mint humbugs.

"There you are," said the kind lady, smiling at her, "All on your own are you?"

"No, my parents are going to meet me later."

She recognised local families and friends meeting together to eat cold beef and pickles, as she headed for the entertainments, where her parents had told her to meet them. When she found them they gave her some money and she went on the roundabout, looked at the animals in the menagerie, and lingered by the dancing-booth, where couples jigged on rickety boards to the fiddle, trombone and harp. Holding on to her father's hand Bertha ventured into the displays of curiosities and saw the freak shows;

"Roll up, roll up and see the fattest lady in the world, dwarfs and the albino with pink eyes."

Music spilled out of every pub; customers refreshed with beer, sang "Farmer's Boy," "Annie Laurie" and "Sweet Marie." The town was full of pleasure-seekers getting a well- earned break from their usual dull, hard working lives.

Meanwhile, her sister Eliza's husband, Henry had decided that there wasn't enough money coming in to feed his growing family now they had three children; he planned to leave Suffolk as so many others had done, and find work in Hertfordshire on an estate, Northaw, only twenty miles from London. The Tudor style house stood at the centre of 250 acres of woodland and had a large garden. Henry had got the job of gardener/groom there by answering an advertisement in the newspaper.

Bertha adored her eldest sister. Whenever Eliza visited the cottage with Henry and the children she always rushed to Bertha and hugged her as if she would never let go. Then Eliza and her mother would sit by the fire chatting, occasionally looking over at her. She would hear the words "De Vere" and "the Hall" mentioned and, in time, began to suspect there was something being kept from her. She tried to work out what they were talking about. But when she asked her mother outright, she grasped her by her shoulders and looked at her intently, saying,

"Eliza used to work up there for a while, that's all, but don't you never say a word about it - do you hear me?"

Bertha mutely nodded her head, too overawed to speak.

Eliza had tears in her eyes as she said goodbye to her family, promising to write. They had to catch the train from Ipswich to London, then another to Potter's Bar. She felt very nervous as she had never been on a train before. How would they manage with three children, aged five, three and one? Would they find a cab to take them from the station with so many people and so much luggage?

She and Henry had packed up most of their things to send ahead - clothes, pots, pans, dishes, sheets and blankets. They sold some things to make money for the journey and gave some things away to Henry's family. Eliza was sorry to see her precious things go. They would have to buy some second hand furniture in Northaw. But Henry's mind was made up that this was best for all of them, so she resolved to put the past behind her. It was another new start for the family.

She packed some bread, cheese and apples for the journey. The horse was harnessed and the boxes and bags piled up on the cart. They all managed to fit in the trap and she was so busy looking after the children and making sure nothing got left behind that she didn't feel sad yet. The station platform at Ipswich was large and so full of people it was a scramble to get aboard with the children and luggage. They found an empty carriage compartment in 3rd class, while the engine hissed and clouds of steam billowed around them.

The guard blew his whistle and the train chuffed grandly out of the station - the adventure had begun! Henry was calm and smiled down at her; she always felt safe with him. The journey was long and they peered out of the window, as the big skies and golden cornfields of Suffolk gradually disappeared into long stretches of countryside which looked unfamiliar.

She'd gazed at the lanes and cottages of home before she left to try and imprint them on her memory.

Would they ever come back or see the family again? She just had to follow where Henry went and hope and pray for the best. When they drew into yet another station, and heard a guard calling "Northaw! Northaw!" Eliza hurriedly gathered the children together to climb down from the train.

From then on Eliza was too busy to be homesick, finding the little row of terraced houses at Gould Pond, settling the children in, lighting a fire and getting some soup with onion, carrot and swede on the range, and arranging where they would all sleep. It was a constant round of unpacking, cooking, child care, cleaning, Henry going off to his new job and finding the local school for little Henry John to start.

In the market, Eliza found tripe, sweetbreads and udder a lot cheaper than at the butcher's. She noticed that the local people were quite friendly to them but spoke in a different dialect which was hard to understand. When they found out that she came from Suffolk, they called her a "Suffolk turnip." She soon put them right on that - "My father is an engine driver and we've been in good service- we're not just country bumpkins, you know."

Gradually they got to know the neighbours and found their feet. One good piece of news was that Eliza's younger sister, Rose was going to come up and see them. She was now twenty years old and in domestic service. Eliza went to meet her at the station,

"What news of Mother and Father and Bertha?"

"They're fine and she's growing up fast. Twelve years old and quite the little lady now."

"Oh, yes, I wish I could see them all. But it's lovely

to see you, Rose, you're so good with the children and a real help in the house. Let's walk up to see Henry at the stables." He was detangling a horse's tail and brushing its coat with linseed oil to make it shine; he said he had already mucked out the stable. Then he went to fetch fresh water and the horse's feed, before leading him gently back to his stall and patting him on the neck. He was able to walk home with them as the master had said he would not be needed again that day.

In Suffolk, Bertha missed her sisters but she found comfort roaming free on the sandy heath; she breathed in the scents of the pink and purple herbs - marjoram, basil, and thyme and listened to the larks singing high overhead. The delicate blue thimbles of harebells mingled with the intense purple of the bellflowers and the heads of self- heal. The blue flowers of the scabious attracted butterflies with their zig- flight, dancing with their mates in the sunshine.

In late summer, yellow predominated; St. John's wort and lady's bedstraw blanketed the area, smelling of honey and new mown grass. The last rock- roses opened on bright days and orange-yellow bird's foot trefoil became long seed pods. There was always a gorse in flower, making the whole area smell of coconut on warm days. If she listened carefully, Bertha could hear the pop of ripe seed pods bursting on the thorny bushes, where warblers, stonechats and linnets nested. Insects fed on the purple heather and sometimes she saw a lizard. These walks always lifted her spirits.

Now she was older, Bertha's class were going to

Snape Old School for some lessons; the boys for woodwork, science and maths and the girls for botany, cookery and needlework. Teacher said "Girls it's very important to be thrifty - to concoct meals out of next to nothing so the men's wages will stretch further. The poor must learn to be less wasteful."

Bertha whispered to her friend Helen,

"That's not true – our mothers know how to cook the food, if only they can get it."

"Quiet, Girls" called out the teacher, "Today you will learn how to bake stuffed hearts, cook vegetables and make semolina pudding - all for 10d. You can show this recipe to your mothers when you get home." Bertha and Helen exchanged glances. The girls also learnt housewifery skills; the textbook said,

> *"Select a house that is well- drained, well-lit and ventilated. Keep the home clean to prevent disease and nurse the sick to health. Keep the family happy at home lest they seek pleasure in objectionable places elsewhere. Be thrifty and save for your old age."*

Objectionable places – does that mean the public house? Thought Bertha, surely no-one would begrudge the menfolk their half pint of beer. We're lucky if we can make ends meet, let alone save up. Most of us have no choice where we live anyway and we've been taught housework by our mothers at home.

In 1902 a new Education Act made provision for secondary schools for working class children to get higher education beyond the age of 13. However, most poor parents couldn't afford to keep their children at school, they needed to earn a living. Bertha was lucky because the De Veres paid for her to go to Grammar School and with the extra tuition she'd received at the Hall, she easily passed the exams.

She'd been able to read books in the old schoolroom there; Grimm's Fairy Tales, Hans Anderson, Lewis Carroll, Sir Walter Scott, and R.L. Stevenson. She loved Dickens, and Tales from the Arabian Nights. Life at the Hall was a magic kingdom of endless play, amusements and pleasure; games of hide and seek among the trees, tea with cakes and glasses of milk, reading beautifully illustrated books in the Library while sunk in a patterned silk sofa.

There she could get lost in a world of her own; her imagination filled with stories of mysterious happenings, exciting adventures, a treasure trove of romance. She was surrounded by beautiful things, antiques, elegant furniture and paintings. Cecilia presided over the large household, governed by good manners. Bertha was aware it was an honour for her to visit there. She wondered why she was welcomed when other village children were completely banned from the house and garden. Sometimes she heard the older servants muttering about "silk purses and sow's ears" and heard the expression "she was no better than she should be" which puzzled her.

She loved the garden, played in the summer house and came to know every tree; the Ilex, the Wellingtonia, and cedar trees on the vast lawn. A path led to the croquet lawn and tennis court. Her kingdom was unlimited for it was the endless fairyland of her imagination.

The children had dogs to accompany them in their games, and cats at the farm. Bertha adored these and they responded to her firm but gentle care. But she and her playmates were country children and not allowed to be sentimental about them. They saw the Keeper going out every day with his gun to shoot rabbits. When Bertha came in through the back door, she turned her eyes away from the game hanging up in the larder outside the kitchen where Cook prepared huge picnic hampers when they went down to the beach. The children were cherished, courteously welcomed everywhere, entertained and protected - enjoying peace and kindness in a safe environment. Conditions that Bertha knew were denied to other children. The architecture, paintings and sculpture influenced their tastes and instilled in them a sense of the past, family identity and pride.

When Bertha stayed overnight, the vast, dark house could be daunting - the staircases and recesses seemed sinister and full of shadows. But the nursery was a safe haven, familiar and homely. Sometimes the bright lights and intimidating conversation of the drawing room were a bit alarming, especially when there were strangers. Cecilia instructed them how to behave when guests were present so they gradually lost their shyness.

"When someone comes into the room for the first time, get up! Shake hands, smile and look them in the eyes when you speak to them."

On wet days, the house became an exciting playground to explore and have lively games. They raced down the corridors and played shuttlecock in the spacious hall.

Nanny and then the Governess taught them the moral values of upper class Christianity; that God had placed everyone in their places and they must keep to them. Self-sacrifice and duty were a naturally accepted part of life which they took with them into adulthood. The boys were encouraged to be brave and independent, but the girls were expected to be quiet and sweet- natured. They must defer to the boys and sacrifice their interests to theirs.

"Don't you envy the boys, Bertha?" asked little Mary, who followed her about adoringly. "They have more freedom and they're more important than us."

"Oh, no" said Bertha, who pitied Lawrence in his green velvet suit with lace collar which was much too restricting for running about the lawn or climbing trees in.

"I want to be like Cecilia when I grow up – I think she's the most wonderful person in the world. Besides I can go where I want at home in the village."

"You are lucky, we're not allowed to go out on our own or play with the village children."

Cecilia did more committee work than her father to do with workhouse conditions, public health, infant mortality and poor housing. Bertha was allowed to sit quietly in the library while Cecilia worked at her desk, writing letters with her white plump hand, so different from her own mother's work-worn one.

"Why are you always so busy, Cecilia?" asked Bertha.

Cecilia stopped writing and looked at her intently before answering

"Our position in society, our power and wealth has been given as a stewardship from God. We must do what we can to relieve sickness and poverty. That's why I've started a coal and clothing club in the village – it's my Christian duty. I add to the small weekly sums, purchase and distribute the goods once a year."

Bertha resolved that she would follow her example when she grew up.

One day she went down to play in the summer house, but stopped when she heard grownup voices coming from inside. Cecelia was talking about her charity work when the Baron interrupted in his loud voice and said,

"Of course we mere men know you women are morally superior with your sympathetic, nurturing natures. Good works are your sphere, aren't they, Frederick?"

"Yes, father, you're right. Ah, by the way, talking of good works, how is the child getting along these days?"

"Very well," said Cecelia, "she's going to the grammar school now."

"Oh, jolly good." Frederick said. He was already planning his trip to Monte Carlo for the clay pigeon shooting.

Bertha always remembered this conversation –but she would not fully realize the significance of it until years later. She walked slowly back up to the house to the kitchen where the housekeeper and cook were organising soup, worn clothing and leftover food ready for Cecilia to take to the poor in the local villages.

The housekeeper was saying, "Miss Cecilia seems

to enjoy meeting the villagers and caring for their needs. And it's a chance for her to use her energy; she's so bright and talented."

"It's a chance to use her power and control over others, you mean" said Cook.

"Well, of course, she is a natural leader" said the housekeeper.

"From what I hear she can be inconsiderate and overbearing" said Cook – "going into cottages without knocking to pry and scold. She's given out some harsh rules - trying to get rid of estate girls whose church-going or general behaviour isn't up to her standards, which is a bit of a joke considering what goes on here during the house parties. What about the time she ordered the school girls' hair to be cut short to prevent head lice? That went down well."

"Well it worked didn't it?" said the housekeeper. "Think of all her charity work; giving balls and garden parties to raise funds. She's the patron of quite a few committees too. Ever since she was a child she's visited the poor with her dear mother- she has their welfare at heart."

Just then Cecilia herself came into the room and Bertha helped her sort out bedding, clothing, food, medicine; gowns and shawls for the women, frocks for Sunday school girls, and layettes for babies. She knew what would be really useful to them.

"Do you think your mother would like this gown, Bertha?" said Cecilia holding it up, and looking at it doubtfully.

"Oh, yes, please, she likes something fancy."

Cecilia had also founded and presided over

Mothers' Meetings to give advice on bringing up children and housekeeping, explaining the virtues of cleanliness and order. Bertha sat with her mother in the back row. Her mother muttered

"What does an old maid like her know about it? That's what I'd like to know."

"Shush, Mother, she has our welfare at heart." replied Bertha, piously repeating what she'd heard the housekeeper say.

She felt so proud when Cecilia came on her regular visits to the school. She paid the poorest children's school fees and awarded prizes for good attendance and behaviour. Taking a special interest in the girls, she made sure that they learnt needlework, laundry and housework, so there would always be a pool of trained domestic servants for the big house in the future and to prepare them for married life. One of the girls asked her if she needed a maid.

"Oh, no my dear, I don't accept inexperienced school leavers for the Hall. But I will help you to find jobs at local farms, vicarages and such."

In 1904, her eldest brother, Frederick, heir to the estate and title, now aged 37, married Lilian, the heiress of a Jamaican sugar plantation. She was 40. Eliza heard the news and retorted

"Well, she's bit long in the tooth, isn't she? I doubt they'll have any children at that age – serve him right. Still she's wealthy of course."

Influenced by the Suffragette movement, women were beginning to insist on their own self-development and equality with men. One of Bertha's school books told stories of famous women, like Florence

153

Nightingale, who was the well- educated daughter of a wealthy landowner with a vocation to become a nurse.

Bertha read about her work in hygiene and elementary care in the Crimean War which had prevented soldiers' deaths from infected wounds. She gazed at a picture of Florence carrying her lamp, doing her ward rounds at Scutari; the caption said,

"her benign presence is an influence for good comfort....she is a ministering angel, as her slender form glides quietly along each corridor, every fellow's face softens with gratitude at the sight of her."

Bertha imagined herself doing the same. Perhaps she could go one of the Nursing schools she had seen advertised in the newspaper to get a certificate? She confided in Cecilia her dreams of becoming a nurse.

"Good idea, Bertha," she said "I've been wondering what to do with you, now that you're leaving school. I shall write to my cousin Adele. She's the matron of a hospital in London. You can go up there to train. Nursing is quite respectable now - it used to be such a lowly job when I was a girl."

Bertha went home to tell her parents the exciting news.

"Our girl a trained nurse in London, fancy that!" said her mother. "We're so proud of you Bertha. But the house will seem empty without you, our last child to leave home. You'd better write to your sisters and tell them the good news."

There was great excitement when the letter came

accepting her as a probationer nurse, enclosing a copy of the rules and regulations, offering a salary of eight pounds per year(increased annually) and giving instructions as to uniform and the date she was to start training. Cecilia ordered her dressmaker to make up her uniform, and Bertha wrote to tell Eliza her good news.

The day before Bertha left, Cecilia said goodbye to her at the Hall. A maid told her to come to the mistress' study. Cecilia was standing in the middle of the room.

"Close the door." She indicated the sofa and settled down in her armchair.

"So you're leaving tomorrow" Cecilia said.

"Yes, that's right." Bertha nodded. It felt strange to think she was with her for the last time, when she had known her since she was a baby.

"Now, Bertha, don't forget the things I have taught you. Always remember your time here. Of course, it will be obvious to people you meet, by your bearing and upbringing, that you are different from other village girls. No need to mention our name or the name of the house, simply say that your father is a farmer and that you were often invited up to the big house to play with the other children."

There was a silence, then she said

"It's been a long time, hasn't it?"

"Yes." Bertha was silent, thinking of all the wonderful times she'd had at the hall.

"Thank-you Cecilia, thank-you for all your kindness to me."

Bertha wanted to fling her arms around her but

knew Cecelia would be horrified – she considered any display of emotion terribly vulgar. Cecilia waved away her thanks.

"I have done my duty as your guardian, that's all." She took a book from a small table. "Here's a little going away present, something to remember us by." It was Miss Nightingale's book on nursing, in a beautiful red leather binding.

Bertha thanked her again, choked with tears. They were now both standing up and the audience was over.

"Take care of yourself." Said Cecelia. Let me know how you're getting on and write if you need anything."

"I will" said Bertha, knowing she probably wouldn't.

"Goodbye then. Good luck". Bertha slipped out of the Hall and the servants waved her goodbye.

Her parents came to the station to see her off. As Bertha sat on the train, she opened her new book and read, *"Nursing is most truly said to be a high calling, an honourable calling."* She felt nervous. Her hands trembled and her heart beat faster. Would she be able to do this? Soon tingling excitement took over from apprehension. It was the start of a great adventure. She was on a railway train, puffing and jolting through the countryside. She had left school, her parents and the village in Suffolk far away. She would be independent and have opportunities never imagined in her family before. She was determined to do well.

On the first morning at the nurses' home, Bertha proudly laid out her new uniform on the bed – but she was all fingers and thumbs as she put on the long blue dress, starched apron, and belt. Someone knocked on the door and the probationer who stood there gave her a sympathetic glance and helped her adjust her cap. They hurried to join the other students assembled in the hall. The faint whiff of ether and carbolic soap pervaded the air, as Matron, clad in black, her pale face framed by a white crimped cap, stood up and surveyed them sternly from the platform at one end of the room. Bertha gazed at her curiously – so this was Cecilia's cousin, Adele.

"Now girls, welcome to St. Thomas's Hospital - as our great founder said, remember work hard during your training to learn and do all things perfectly. The honour does not lie in merely putting on your uniform. Honour lies in loving perfection, consistency, and in working hard and patiently for it; do not say 'how clever I am!' but 'I am not yet worthy', and will live to deserve to be called a Trained Nurse."

Her voice droned on and on, but Bertha lost track of what she was saying as she gazed at the full length portrait of Florence Nightingale on the wall behind her and daydreamed about her new life…

She was therefore startled at the end of the session when a probationer told her to report to Matron's office. She followed the girl and stood as straight and tall as she could while Matron looked her up and down.

"I do hope you realize, Miss Stone, that you will be treated in exactly the same way as the other probationers during your training here?"

Bertha felt like a country simpleton cut down to size, but she stood up for herself.

"Yes, Matron, I want to do something worthwhile

with my life – to look after the sick and learn to do it properly."

An almost human smile flitted across the impassive mask of Matron's face.

"Very well, you may go to your duties now."

The senior probationer nurse took Bertha to Men's medical Ward. The sink room was where they collected bedpans and wash basins. The smell of disinfectant there was overpowering.

"Hurry up with washing the patients, we have to start bed-making next," she said.

It was awkward dealing with naked men. Bertha was grateful when one of them, seeing her embarrassment, said kindly

"Just give me the flannel, Nurse, and I'll do the rest."

At least she had been to school with boys and seen animals in the farmyard, unlike some of the girls there who'd been kept cloistered at home in the schoolroom with a governess.

As Bertha tucked in the last bed corner, a trolley was wheeled onto the ward and she had to take the meals round, carefully checking the list of special diets. That first day seemed endless as she struggled to keep up with facts, impressions and fears. As she hung up the last scrubbed rubber sheet and returned the final clean spit mug to its locker top, she sighed wearily and joined the other nurses going off to nine o'clock supper. Women were expected to be delicate without much appetite or energy, but student nurses certainly had. She sat on her bed rubbing her aching feet and tense back, before falling into a deep sleep.

"Six o'clock, Nurse!" someone banged on her door next day.

And fortified with kippers and hot tea, she was soon back on the ward. The men greeted her and she felt needed. As it was doctor's day, the big boss came round with his crowd of young men in white coats and stethoscopes, to prod and discuss the patients' bodies. After her two hour break, she came back in time to help serve out the mince and potatoes for the patients' lunch. Then it was time to tidy the ward for the weekly visiting hour. She had to stand guard at the door to take parcels brought in, for sister to inspect later. When the visitors had gone, she learned how to take temperatures and check pulses, using the new watch from her uniform pocket, feeling very efficient and important.

After a week or two, things became easier. She made friends and got to know the patients. At the visiting hour, she was amused when a patient's wife tried to smuggle in pickled pork for her husband. Sister snatched it off her and confiscated it at once.

"Aw, Sister, 'e does love 'is pickles, you're starving 'im in 'ere!"

"My good woman, you'll kill him - he's on a special diet - he's got a gastric ulcer!"

The sitting room was warm, and, when the student nurses were off duty, Sister often gave lectures there while they took notes on bandaging and physiology, aided by Lucy the anatomical doll and Jimmy the skeleton.

Death was the invisible enemy they were trained to fight, made more difficult by the fact that no one knew where the majority of illnesses came from. Most of it was blamed on bad air and smells. However, closed windows could trap germs inside - TB spread like that - and Miss Nightingale's rules said the windows were to be opened on the wards most nights of the year.

But death was a regular visitor just the same. One morning Bertha came on duty to find screens round one of the beds. She could hear the night staff and Sister inside, conferring over the rattling breaths of a dying man. This cast a gloom over her morning chores, but her colleague told her

"Cheer up, Bertha, you'll get used to it."

Then the painful breathing stopped and the hissing gas cylinder was turned off. Staff nurse called to Bertha,

Will you help, please?"

She had to steel herself to go behind those screens and undress the poor man. He was still warm. At least he had died in his bed, cared for, his passing eased in every possible way. Later she helped put his body into a calico shroud. With quick efficient hands the other nurse bandaged the sagging jaw and closed the staring eyes, weighting them with penny coins.

"There, well done, Bertha, we all have to go through it," she said.

Not only did the nurses have to fight disease but they had very little to fight it with. On the TB Ward, the patients were emaciated and drawn. When they coughed up blood all the staff could offer was a dose of linctus. The only treatment was good food, fresh air and rest. To some patients, death came as a friend.

Bertha felt depressed and longed for her weekend

off, which was from 6pm Saturday to 10pm Sunday once a month. There wasn't time to go home and she tried to get some rest as she had been posted to night duty next, but it was hard to sleep with constant footsteps outside and bright sunlight coming through the window blind. She seemed to have only just dropped off to sleep when the knock on the door came,

"Seven o'clock, Nurse."

But the move to the gynaecological ward meant a step up, for there she carried out some treatments, like enemas and douches. She joined the queue for night rations then walked down to the ward which was dark except for the shaded lamp on sister's desk. Night staff nurse directed her to prepare breakfast trays, while she did her round.

Setting the trays; cleaning bowls, basins, sinks, scrubbing shelves and rubber sheets; polishing sterilizing drums kept her busy until about midnight. She was not allowed to sit down or be idle, so began sewing stiff calico shrouds. She wondered when she would be a proper nurse like her heroine. Drowsiness came over her, she kept nodding off, but she was determined to keep going. Hot buttered toast, tea and a rissole kept her spirits up. As she looked down onto the dark street below, all was quiet and only the footsteps of a patrolling policeman and the far off rumble of traffic broke the silence. She wondered when she could rise above the constant scrubbing, dusting and polishing to be a proper nurse. Still, the exams came up in the autumn and if she studied hard, she could pass and move on.

Babies began to cry as dawn broke. The street woke

into life and the ward round of washing and bedpans started. She helped to hand out breakfasts of bread and margarine with mugs of tea. Her own meal was mutton and rice pudding in the back to front world of night duty.

After night duty, Bertha was sent to Casualty, where she had heard the Sister in charge was very strict. As she nervously surveyed the huge waiting room furnished with wooden benches and bordered by small cubicles, a small figure suddenly came out of nowhere,

"Well don't just stand there, get on and scrub that table, Nurse. You're not just an ornament I hope, you're here to work."

"Yes, Sister."

Half an hour of hot soapy water and brush later, she returned to assist the specialists by setting out their tables with the correct instruments, in the correct place, or else. She brought in the patients and chaperoned the female ones. Then she boiled all the instruments in enamel sterilisers over a gas ring. She dared not put a foot wrong and hoped Sister would write her a good report when she left Casualty two weeks later.

The weather got colder, but as Christmas drew nearer it brought a true spirt of goodwill to the hospital; all the staff were united in a fellowship of loving and giving. Bertha was making paper-chains with Ward 8 staff when Sister came in with a bottle of sherry from Matron.

"Pull out the cork and get some glasses, Nurse Stone" she smiled at her, "And we'll celebrate."

On Christmas morning the tree was hung with presents for the patients. The consultant Physician dressed up as Santa to give them out. Another senior doctor carved the turkey for patients' dinner and then the nurses went round the wards singing carols, like angels in long blue cloaks. Matron popped in, in unusual good humour, to cast a motherly eye over everything.

Bertha found that she was better educated than the girls who had been taught by a Governess, as she had been to grammar school. However her hand still shook when she wrote answers to the questions in the exam that autumn. The viva voce next day was even worse; a doctor sat there with Lucy the china doll, and asked her to point out the liver. Thankfully his moustache outlined a fatherly smile at her answer. All the probationers passed and Bertha was thrilled to receive a parcel containing the blue and white striped material for her new junior staff nurse's uniform.

The housemen and students now treated her with new respect, but flirted with her if Sister wasn't around. Some of them tried to hold her hand while she was assisting, watching her every movement with admiring glances. But Bertha was conscious of her new responsibility and status and got on with her work.

She had other things to think about. Such as what was she going to do after her finals at the end of her third year?

British trained nurses were greatly in demand; she could apply for jobs in hospitals, or workhouse infirmaries all over Britain. New hospitals were being built; often specialising in the treatment of particular groups of patients such as children, cancer patients, and ear, nose and throat sufferers.

She received her final certificate from Matron, who unbent enough to say

"You're a credit to the family."

She was a qualified nurse – a lady of the lamp at last. Yet as she went down the steps of the hospital away from the smell of ether and carbolic she felt a great sadness.

Chapter Nine - Decline and Fall

Meanwhile in Northaw, Eliza was fighting her own battle against disease; there had been a case of scarlet fever at the school a few days previously and her daughter, Hilda Rose now five, had developed a sudden temperature and vomited.

"It hurts, Mum!" she cried, pointing at her throat. Eliza looked down her open mouth and saw that the tonsils were filmy white – O, God, help her - she knew that meant scarlet fever. She pressed her reddened skin and it stayed white for several minutes. Desperate, she sent Henry for the doctor.

He shook his head and confirmed the disease.

"You must keep the other children away from her and not let them mix with other children". Eliza started to pant with fear, but Henry put his arm around her shoulders to calm her. "Don't worry, love, I'll ask if the neighbour can have them for a bit."

Next day, a red rash covered the little girl's body and Eliza sat with her all day, soothing her hot forehead with a cold flannel till she slept. Then she had a swollen tongue and couldn't swallow. Soon the skin would start to peel, but she was already weaker, her face pale; she couldn't even take a sip of water. Eliza sat up all night with her. Henry stayed with them, praying, but in the morning the little body was lifeless, already cold and pale.

Eliza felt exhausted and heart broken. And all the time she was so tired, too tired to struggle. Only the sight of her two sons' sad little faces looking at her from the bedroom door wakened her to her responsibilities. She beckoned to them and they walked uncertainly to her, looking down at the motionless body of their sister on the bed. She hugged them close and told them Hilda had gone up to heaven to be with the angels, where they would all meet again one day.

The body was kept in the parlour for a week before the funeral and all the neighbours came in. Everyone in the street drew their curtains as a sign of respect. They were so kind, bringing gifts of food and sitting with Eliza. The expense of the funeral was a worry on top of the grief at losing their child but they used all their savings to pay for a coffin with a white satin lining and a proper burial. She couldn't kiss her goodbye, for fear of infection. She just whispered through her tears that she loved her.

The comforting words of the funeral service "there shall be no more cold and hunger or weeping" helped Eliza and Henry through. The doctor was kind, "You have other children – they need you more than ever," but little fair haired Hilda would no longer dance like a sunbeam through their lives.

Afterwards, Eliza was in a daze for weeks and she wondered if she was to blame - had her sin of having an illegitimate child brought this sorrow on them? Had God punished her for having Bertha outside wedlock by taking her legitimate daughter? She sat in the church - she loved to hear the singing. It was so peaceful and pleasant to shut her eyes and pray. The curate found her there and she told him her story. He was sympathetic, even indignant.

"If your daughter had been better fed and better

housed, she might have lived! The upper classes have a moral duty to make amends for preying sexually and economically on the working classes. Society may pass a sentence of utter, final excommunication on fallen women, but the Church does not. Women like you are not at all worse than ordinary women of the servant class…far more often sinned against than sinning; you did not sin alone, yet bear on earth the burden of the guilt, cast forth to utter despair."

"Thank you Reverend," Eliza said, drying her tears. It was a relief to have confessed and she felt much better than she had for years.

She wrote to her mother on black-edged paper to tell her the sad news.

Down in Suffolk, Cecilia was bored and restless. Now in her forties, she realised she was the last child at home and would never marry. She missed Bertha, and her other nephews and nieces were grown up and had lives of their own. But she still had her duties to carry out as mistress of De Vere Hall.

She held a dinner party on the eve of the general election. The guests included a diplomat home on leave and women famous for their beauty or wit, who either made sparkling conversation or were wise enough not to interrupt the men's talk but sat looking statuesque or flowerlike. When the correct moment came, after supper, Cecilia rose magnificently and signalled to the ladies. They retired to the drawing room with a swish of silk skirts and perfume, and left the gentlemen to their port, cheroots and rude stories.

The ladies arranged themselves about the room and chatted about local matters and amusing gossip.

Frederick, Cecelia's brother, was present, talking to Cabinet Ministers, and high officials from far off places in the Empire, who were keen to make the government realise the difficulties of their position. The pattern of Freddie's life had been set before he was born; prep school, Eton, Oxford, The Guards, love affairs with fashionable married women, visits to wealthy houses, Court functions, engagement to a suitable lady, marriage in the chapel, children, more affairs, speeches in the House of Lords; after dinner talk about Reform and the growth of democracy - worried but not seriously disturbed. On 12th of August, shooting began, then hunting and fishing; photograph in the illustrated papers propped on a shooting stick with two dogs and a loader; upon death, borne to the family vault on a farm cart, with employees and tenants standing by, their heads bowed and caps in hand.

The De Veres had held on to political power and social superiority until now. They were the Government. However, the Baron was seriously worried about the political situation.

"Remember the French Revolution," he said, "the shadow of the guillotine hangs over us...." the shadow deepened and the nobility were being attacked in Parliament. There was unrest in the country; the old order of things was changing. The Government had to concede reforms, giving more men the vote.

In the village on the day of the general election, little school work was done because the children could hear bands of voters passing below the windows and shouts of "Evans for freedom! He be the boy for the farm labourer!" The children were uneasy because they knew their fathers were voting for the Liberal candidate and the teacher was wearing a blue rosette which proclaimed her for the big house and the rectory and against the villagers. They were not allowed to wear red for the Liberal cause but most carried a bit of red material to wear going home and a couple of bold girls sported red ribbons in their hair.

The teacher went to the window to watch people going by. She said pointedly "Now here are two men wearing blue going to vote for law and order – respectable, quiet men. They were servants of the parson and the squire. The children resented this, but cheered up when she announced "You can go home at three o'clock as its election day". It was a pity she added "but be careful, there may be drunken men about".

The edifice of society stood apparently sound but undermined already. It couldn't survive in a changing world, where machines did what men and horses had done and the luxuries of the few were becoming available to the majority. Some of the old women still curtsied to the gentry, but younger women just gave a smile and quick nod of the head. They had ambition and paid no attention to the older ones claim "I know my place and that's good enough for me."

Change came slowly, but it came. The younger villagers had better education, were a little better off but though they were modest and kind, they felt a growing sense of injustice and questioned "When will we get a fair share of the fruits of our labour?" A weekly newspaper came into every house, bought or borrowed, and ideas about social justice and the rights of the people were slowly percolating. "It must be true", they said to each other, "it's there in black and white".

Bertha's mother seldom discussed politics except to say "Why can't Father leave such things alone? Tis no business of his- who cares who governs? Whoever it is they won't give us nothing and they can't take anything from us, as we haven't got anything! Why vote Liberal when it's the gentry, the Conservatives that give coal or a blanket at Christmas. We're powerless; it's a case of "them" and "us"; the masters were born to rule and we to follow. That don't include the new rich, mind – they're only tradesmen trying to be gentry".

Bertha's father argued with her "the farmer pays starvation wages all year and thinks he makes up for it by giving them one good meal a year at harvest. And that goes for the people at the big house – a few treats at Christmas, and charity handouts – it's not enough!"
Everyone was waiting for the results to come in. The votes were counted. The people had the right to be heard and now they had spoken. It was a Liberal landslide.

The Baron had lost his seat! His own people; tenants and villagers had elected Evans, a man with no land, an outsider - after all the Baron had done for them. It was a terrible shock.

Bertha was sorry for him and Eliza felt guilty that

her curse on the family still seemed to be having an effect.

Yet, sitting alone in his study during the next few days, the Baron had to admit that, in a way, he was relieved that he was no longer a Member of Parliament - the House of Commons was no longer a country gentlemen's club, filled with likeminded people. There was a new breed of hard- nosed men there now – working men in cloth caps and tweeds, solicitors, financiers, business men like W.H.Smith, a station bookseller! Parliament lacked the gentlemanly refinement of the old days. Lately it had become a bear pit of violent, uncalled for, unjust attacks on the landowners and old titled families.

And the false heartiness of electioneering nowadays was quite distasteful. The hand shaking, back-slapping, baby-kissing! He'd been pushed about from place to place, not his own master, but made to make many speeches a day and above all, told never to lose his temper, but to keep smiling at all times. Not to mention the expense! He could no longer afford the donations to local charities, the church repairs, alterations to the hospital, contributions to the football and cricket clubs and the friendly societies required.

Comfortable evenings at home had to give way frequently to village hall gatherings, Primrose League meetings for Tory ladies, political meetings in schools, sometimes only attended by a dozen yokels, two or three women and a little boy…it made life impossible. He refused to stand anymore. He would retire. Let them take on foreigners and carpet baggers with no family or business links to the seat, or Middle class outsiders - journalists, lawyers, tradesmen.

Ever since the agricultural depression in the 1870s, tenants had blamed him. They said rents were too high. He discussed all this with his agent. "Then that young Welsh upstart, what was his name? Lloyd-George, introduced death duties which were punitive, punitive, just wooing the masses."

"My land is no longer my wealth and power, but a millstone around my neck. I've already started to sell off some outlying areas," the Baron said to his Agent.

"But I suppose we must show willingness to compromise in the spirit of the age," he sighed wearily.

The Baron had done his best to maintain and raise the family's position, but he'd had to take out mortgages to do it and the interest on them and other loans consumed a large proportion of his income. He had crippling debts, fixed outgoings and taxes were going up.

He couldn't understand where he had gone wrong. Living in his country house, protected by high walls, with servants to free him from distractions, he'd helped run the nation and maintained the vast self-sufficient estate for guests, and the family.

He'd ruled the neighbourhood, like his father before him, through public service; the law court, control of the school and the church.

Yes, he'd always attended church on Sunday – the rector, younger son of an aristocratic family, to whom he'd given the living, never preached a change in social relations; he attacked the sinners, he didn't say society was responsible. He said class differences were

God's will. He reminded the congregation of the responsibilities of the ruling class –

"They pay taxes, sit on the bench, oversee their estate, keep up their position by entertaining guests – could you do it? No, thank God you have other skills and the strength to do your work. So be content, work hard, show respect to your elders and betters."

He'd gone quite red in the face as he warmed to his theme, the Baron remembered. And finished by saying,

"The doctrine of universal brotherhood is a delusion!"

How he boiled up in anger after Polling Day, his eyes flashing. He thrust himself over the edge of the pulpit and shouted "Some of you have lately forgotten your duty and we know the cause, the Radical cause!"

From now on the Baron would stick to local government, council and JP work. Shopkeepers might get places on the council but he greeted his fellow councillors with patrician courtesy, including a man who'd turned out to be the porter! Well, it was hard to tell nowadays.

He was being pushed aside by plutocrats - manufacturers, brewers, financiers, Americans. They bought peerages, and bought up country estates for their weekends and shooting parties. Well he wouldn't call on them.

They were pleasure- seeking, materialistic and extravagant. Because of their money, some people tolerated them.

Now he might be forced to let out his London house, or even sell it. Freddie would have to take paid work. How was he going to break it to him?

The next day he summoned the Agent to his study and had an unpleasant morning going through the accounts with his sons. They found that a most unsatisfactory state of affairs existed. The agent spoke,

"Your Lordship, the everyday expenses must be reduced; these are your options; curtail the hunting, let or give up the London house, cut the season from five months to two, drink less alcohol, let out the country house and the shooting, dismiss some of the servants. Sell some of the paintings and books. Sell land and buy stocks and shares."

The Baron objected strongly "One doesn't want to go down in history as losing our old family possessions, but the state has turned hostile – we're under attack! We'll be lucky if we can keep a tomb over our heads at this rate!"

"There's no room for sentiment, Your Lordship. We must be rational and calculate our investments."

"But there's no demand for land! Prices are so low, we must hold on in the hope of better times."

After some persuasion he agreed to certain things which they hoped would put matters right, for a time at any rate. Having to regulate expenditure was very unpleasant.

"Someone in the family has to make some money!" He hated the situation but accepted it.

Freddie said "You're not going to sell all our family treasures, are you Father?"

The Baron felt the disapproving eyes of his ancestors' portraits looking down on him. Where were the certainties of the past, when he knew what he was and where he was going? He'd planted trees he'd hoped his grandchildren would see flourish.

"What does the future hold now?" he said, "We're prisoners of time – change is afoot, our family as landed aristocrats is coming to an end, and our England with it. How easily these financial difficulties could be overcome, boys if you'd married American heiresses!" He attempted a feeble joke.

"Oh, I think they set their caps higher than us," said Freddie "they want to marry Dukes and Earls!" They all laughed uneasily, trying to put a brave face on the situation.

So what they had bought from penniless continental aristocrats they now had to sell to new American millionaires. The man from Christie's arrived a few days later.

He smiled broadly and shook hands. The Baron disliked him from the start, thinking all those teeth made him look like a wolf. But he merely said

"I hope we can do business."

The man picked up a spindly chair and turned it over, "Very nice, very nice, good quality."

Then he went all over the house, touching all his things, writing in a little notebook. Finally he shook hands in the hall and went out to his big shiny car, black shoes flashing as he got in and drove away.

Well that's a relief he thought, that wasn't too bad. But a week later, a huge van came, wheels crunching on the gravel. Five men got out and came into the house. They picked up some chairs and carried them out to the huge van. It took two at either end to take the sofas and larger objects. They took so much. The rooms looked empty, the walls had bare patches. They wrapped ornaments in a cloth and put them in a box. Then they rolled up some carpets and took them out. They even got a ladder and loosened one of the chandeliers before removing it.

"I hope you won't miss these treasures too much", the wolf man said.

"Thank-you," said the Baron, through clenched teeth.

"Thank-you – the pleasure's all mine, I assure you," he smiled again. "I have many American clients keen to buy antiques, especially French ones. They like to buy history, they have so little."

"Plunderers!" muttered the Baron.

But it still wasn't enough; "Freddie, you'll have to start earning your own living as well as Percy and Hugh."

"What me! But, Father, I'm the eldest – I'm the heir to your title, estate and fortune. What's left of it. What you haven't spent entertaining royalty and breeding horses!"

"Frederick, have some respect for your father!" interrupted the Agent. But Freddie went on

"It's not what I've been brought up to expect. What can I do? I know more about spending money than making it!" He got up and left the room, slamming the door behind him.

"Shall I go to him, Father?" said Percy.

"No, leave him alone. He needs time to adjust."

Frederick went straight upstairs to the attic to find Nanny in her cosy room. He didn't speak but knelt beside her chair, put his head in her lap and sobbed. She put her hand on his back and patted it as she had when he was a child.

"Now, now, all will come right in the end, you'll see."

Frederick couldn't avoid the awkward confrontation with his Father forever. He kept out of his way as much as possible, but one evening, the Baron called him into his study.

"Freddie, have a cigarette in here, won't you?"

"It's beastly late," he replied uneasily, "I was just going to bed."

"I shan't keep you long," said the Baron.

Each dreaded the coming interview.

The study table was littered with account books, letters and piles of old Punch magazines. It brought back memories of school holidays, asking for more pocket money, going over school reports, and that terrible row when he'd had to give up Eliza.

"I think we'd better talk a little about money matters," said the Baron, "I did say that you would have to find paid employment. Let's go over the options together."

"As far as that's concerned, I'm the heir."

"I'm afraid you won't come into anything like the fortune I inherited, what with taxation, cost of living, the agricultural depression and so on. You have to face the fact that you won't be a rich man, but a poor one. You must make your own way."

"What do you suggest?"

"Well, the usual I suppose. What about the Army, Navy, Public Service, the learned professions, the Church?"

"You're out of date, Father, they have competitive

exams now; they're crowded with applicants. Middle class public schoolboys – they're good at passing exams, damned swots."

"What about a court appointment? I know a clerk at Privy Council who still has three days hunting a fortnight. He doesn't work fulltime of course, he's got other things to do, like writing books about his ancestors and cricket."

"They don't want genteel dilettantes anymore." Freddie sighed. "There's been a revolution in the corridors of power, as well as on the land." He drew on his cigarette.

The Baron flinched with pain at the memory of his recent political defeat.

"Well, the Law has great social prestige; it's the best preparation for a political career, good training for administering an estate and sitting on the bench. Your good connections will help you obtain briefs and secure promotion and you can enjoy a congenial lifestyle."

"They have bar exams now, Father." Frederick blew out a cloud of smoke.

"Well, what about the church?"

"I'm not particularly religious, as you know…"

"That doesn't matter – you'll have a large rectory and a guaranteed income for life. Bishops need social position. You would associate with other county gentry and have time to hunt and shoot. Squire, parson and tenants – the best society known to man."

Frederick shook his head, "Nowadays you need professional vocational training."

"Well then, there's the Army, like your brother

Hugh. An occupation of courage, and leadership. The horsemanship and shooting you've learned on the estate. Gentleman first, officer second, what?"

"I'd want a thousand pounds to buy the uniform and a horse, but the salary's meagre – it costs £600 more than that a year to live. Although Hugh's soldiering does seem to be an endless round of parties, polo and fun with his friends…"

"Or there's the Navy" the Baron moved on quickly, "long spells at sea, of course, distant postings, sailing and navigation are not exactly country skills, except on yachts of course, but we had crew to do all that." The Baron smiled ruefully.

"You forget Radical Jack Fisher – middle class – every fit boy should have his chance. Training together to break down class barriers."

"All this bureaucracy, specialization, expertise," the Baron sighed.

"Yes, Father, society is rather complicated now, knowledge is more detailed, the old amateur attitudes no longer suffice. Jobs require full time workers, imagination, study."

"So what can you do? That only leaves business and finance."

"What!"

"That's how we made our money, my boy. We were in the West Indian sugar trade, growing rich on the sweet tooth of England. Before that we were bankers, using the money we brought out of our French estates." The Baron had meant to be gentle, but now he spoke sharply.

"Look, you have an urgent need to find money; a

position in a mercantile or trading house, apprentice to merchants or stockbrokers to learn a trade."

"Trade!" exclaimed Freddie. "All the commercial things we most detest; business and finance capital. It's distasteful and embarrassing. But if you're going to play the heavy father, I suppose I must."

"If you're wise and lucky," said the baron, "you could secure an income that will enable you to lead at least the façade of landed life. I'll speak to my wine merchant about taking you on in the morning – you're a connoisseur of good wine and port - that should be a good starting point."

Gossip flew round the village about the sale of De Vere treasures and worse than that – the baron's eldest son and heir having to get a job and work for his living. Eliza thought of Freddie's pride and upbringing and pitied him.

The new Labour Party started a Sunday school in the village, and adult and discussion classes. The party released a flood of leaflets and journals which fuelled the flames of political arguments about democracy in the pub.

"We must have social justice, the people have the right to be heard."

In 1906, the papers printed the news that the Labour party had joined with the Liberals and won a landslide victory against the Conservatives. Lloyd George was given the post of Chancellor of the Exchequer and introduced reforms of the Poor Law, so that "the shadow of the workhouse be lifted from the homes of the poor."

Bertha's mother had to eat her words about the Liberals, as she and Father went down to the post office in the village to collect their five shillings a week pension.

"God bless, that Lord George," she said, "he's a real gent. I'll take some flowers from the garden to thank that kind girl behind the counter."

Worse was to come for the baron and his friends. To pay for these pensions, Lloyd George announced his "People's Budget"; increases in taxation, higher death duties on wealthy estates and taxes on profits from the ownership and sale of property. The Baron lamented "I've become a mere tax collector for the Government!"

But for the people, Labour Exchanges were set up and a children's allowance on income tax. And he cut the lifetime of a parliament from seven years to five.

The baron's friend, King Edward V11 died on 6th May 1910. The new King George V didn't like Americans – he held a sober respectable court. Anyway some of the otherworldly gloss had come off the aristocratic life for the heiresses. If their husbands had to go to work every day, they might as well stay home and marry American men. The party was over.

The Baron missed him, although the cost of entertaining him had been a heavy burden. At the funeral, Caesar, his fox terrier, followed the gun carriage led by a highland servant. Eliza saw the photograph in the papers and remembered meeting him and his little dog all those years ago when she was a servant at De Vere Hall. She heard about the continuing decline and fall of the family at De Vere

Hall with mixed emotions; it couldn't be her curse that was causing their misfortunes. The tide of life had turned against them.

Lloyd George's 1911 National Insurance Act gave workers a contributory system of insurance against illness and unemployment. Free medical care, including medicine, was given and a guaranteed pay, when unemployed. Another step towards his goal of "ridding society of poverty and squalor, and the wretchedness and human degradation which always follows it."

But for Cecelia it meant form filling, paperwork and sticking stamps to pay 3d a week for each member of staff as her employer contribution.

"When the old master/ servant relationship always worked perfectly well!" she complained to the Baron.

That autumn she saw him spent a lot of time looking out of the window at the leaves falling in the avenue or sleeping in his armchair. Money was short so her pin money allowance was cut and she had to curtail her charity work. The hunters were sold. She would never hunt again.

He insisted on saving on lighting and coal, so she spent tedious evenings wrapped in a shawl, while the Baron slept over his newspaper, waiting to go up to bed. He told her to give up parties and not to invite people to the house.

"Everyone is in London anyway or abroad," she said. Abroad... She sighed for a big hotel, palm court, band, lounge, lovely shops, smart people, sunshine... But she couldn't leave father. People no longer sought them out as good times were no longer to be expected from them.

Father had dropped out of local interests; the bench, county business, even his own circle was forgetting him. The butler gazed down the avenue longing to see a visitor. If one did call, the Baron was engaged and could see no one.

She couldn't bear to see him like that, pining had made him poorly. He was even a little unkempt, she saw with a pang. His money worries put a great strain on him, aged him. One day, he came to her walking unsteadily,

"I want to go for a walk to see how the young larches are getting on."

The dogs picked up the mood of pleasure. She walked slowly with him. But the next day he stayed in bed.

The news of his illness spread far and wide. The front door began to ring again. The butler received messages of sympathy, inquirers and callers. A fellow councillor told Cecilia

"We've had resolutions at the bench and the council. That will please you – it was heart-warming how the Labour fellows spoke of him. A real English gentleman they said."

Cecelia avoided the village now. There was gossip in the shop, servants' prattle – the universal pity was unbearable.

"What a terrible change in your father, Miss De Vere" people said.

All the family arrived and the Baron sent for Freddie. "It's your high duty to work for the conservation of the estate and the permanence of the family; take part in the public life of your country. I want my epitaph to be - he loved this place."

After his death, the will was read. Naturally, Freddie inherited the title, estates and most of the money. Cecilia received an annuity and bought a house in Sunningdale, Berkshire, near the golf course. The faithful housekeeper also received an annuity, a reward for her long service. Hugh, the youngest son, now a Major serving in India, was provided for. Estate death duty had to be paid on the estate.

"Thanks to that damned Welsh solicitor, Lloyd George," muttered Freddie.

Cecelia had to make way for the new Baroness, now mistress of the hall, her brother's wife, Lilian. It was she who now rose to lead the ladies out of the dining room, who had the keys of the house. The old pace and pattern of the house changed. She took charge and ordered that certain rooms be shut up, rubbish burned, letters opened and bills paid.

"It's all so simple," she said. All was becoming clean, tidy, and mended. The old regime of losing everything and muddling was gone. She was bright and detached, after all it wasn't her old childhood home.

Cecelia suddenly realized that the last week before her departure had come and she had not sorted out her own rooms.

"Could you manage it today?" asked Lilian.

She shrank from the task, but her maid helped her to sort out her wardrobe.

"Put away everything but the black, and the jet. Then later on I'll need the half-mourning…. the purple and mauve."

The maid wrapped everything else she wanted in tissue paper and packed them in labelled boxes. Cecelia told her

"Dispose of those clothes and ornaments, I shan't need them again."

But the accumulation of trifles in her drawers...She dreaded the memories they would evoke; her heart was frozen now, but the theatre programmes, letters, menus, were all relics of a life that was over and gone.

Now she was free of her responsibilities, she needed something as different from this life as possible. Real laughter, not just keeping one's spirits up - to feel young again. But her youth was past. In the mirror she looked worn and lined. She'd lost the bloom of beauty, but she would learn to live again, make a new start.

She heard the stable clock strike early dawn. She started throwing letters on the fire. It's gone, gone forever. At last it was finished. She opened the window and looked out at the sky and breathed the cold November air. Later, Lilian tapped at the door.

"Can I help, dear? The car will be here presently."

Cecelia was irritated beyond endurance by the tone of her voice.

"No thank you."

Then, later, after breakfast, Lilian said

"The motor's waiting."

"Is it?"

Cecelia's last pangs of leaving were submerged in mutual irritation.

The servants were crying in the hall. Determined

not to show any emotion she came down the great staircase, smiling brightly, and swept past everyone waiting with a cheerful "Goodbye" and a wave of her hand. The chauffeur was in the drive with the car door open. He helped her in and they drove away.

The new Baron and Baroness were not involved in the lives of the servants, or "domestic staff" as they insisted on calling themselves now. They were aloof, less concerned with noblesse oblige, more interested in their own pleasure. They enjoyed the new sports of golf and polo, going out in the motor car, easier travel to Europe, the benefits of the telephone. Freddie was not an imperious, pious patriarch like his father. He was more liberal in his attitudes. They had to spend most of their time in London anyway because of his business interests in the wine trade. His impeccable connections meant he never lacked for customers. He was a brilliant salesman. No-one could resist his charm and aristocratic good looks.

It was more difficult to get servants. The villagers looked in the papers for more attractive jobs in offices, shops and factories.

One young girl shocked the housekeeper at her interview,

"I don't believe in cringing, I've got my rights. And I shall need time off of an evening. We're just as good as they are. I refuse to be looked down on or treated like a machine."

The housekeeper had to take her on, no-one else had applied for the job.

Stories about the goings- on at the Hall circulated around the village and Eliza read her mother's letters with amazement and told Henry

"Things have certainly changed since our day – we knew our place then."

Although Freddie offered more free time, outings, attractive servants' quarters and central heating, plumbing, electricity, washing machines and vacuum cleaners meant less work for the maids, the younger servants still skipped off at a moment's notice, complaining

"This place is at the back of beyond."
The windows no longer gleamed, nor the silver. China got broken and the food was badly cooked. The servants were not as efficient or devoted as in the past. Lilian was fretful, Freddie morose as they drank soup the cook had over salted. The butler shambled shakily round the table spilling wine on the cloth.

"He'll have to go." Lilian said.

"But he's been with us so long." Protested Freddie.

"Too long." Lilian's word sounded final.

When they were invited to wealthy neighbours' houses; they loved the champagne, delicious food, and cigars. It was like old times to see things properly done. It made them more impatient with the poverty of the old house. As rising taxes cut into the household budget, and servants' wages rose steadily, Freddie replaced the footmen with cheaper parlour maids and engaged a cook- housekeeper.

The gardens looked neglected, with few flowers, and weeds in the drive. The topiary morphed into the strange shapes that Eliza's husband had dreamed of making years ago. In his day, the family didn't want to see the gardeners – now they were lucky to find one.

They couldn't keep up the kitchen garden or the glasshouses that had been so essential in the past. It was let out to a local market gardener, who supplied the house with fruit and vegetables.

Lilian spent a lot of time discussing the servant problem with her friends.

"I put it down to too much education of the lower orders."

"I find fewer servants get through more work" her friend replied, "Less of them milling around, gossiping and making work for each other."

Thankfully, Lilian could buy more things in the shops, so they didn't need so many staff; food, beverages, linens and cleaning materials were now mass produced. Department stores and mail order delivered goods and services by rail. She ordered in bulk from Fortnum and Masons and had things sent down. The bakery, and brewery supplied the bread and beer. The Laundry collected and delivered the washing. She could telephone agencies if she needed temporary staff or hire waiters for special events. In London, catering firms managed her social functions in fashionable hotels and restaurants.

They still held occasional country house parties at De Vere Hall.

"Do you really keep shops, Lord De Vere...? asked a young house guest, greatly daring.

"Yes, you wouldn't be here if I didn't. Maybe you think it beneath my dignity to work, but I'm not ashamed of earning a living or a flourishing business made by myself. We're not all idle drones, you know." He laughed it off, making a mental note never to invite her again.

Chapter Ten - Herne Bay

Bertha was now a qualified SRN. She applied for a job working at a private nursing home in Herne Bay, a popular seaside resort on the Kent coast. Now aged seventeen, she was tall, with thick chestnut hair and green eyes. Her upbringing and nurse's training had given her confidence and poise. She stood upright and carried herself well. Her voice was gentle and she was charming and gracious to everyone.

As she stepped down from the train she breathed in the clean, salty air, refreshing after the stuffiness of London. Having asked directions to the nursing home, she realised she had some time to spare, and walked on the promenade, in bright sunlight, while screaming gulls wheeled overhead. Fashionable people were strolling along, past the tall houses, hotels and guesthouses. Ahead was a tall clock tower, pointing high into the blue sky. A steam- boat was docking at the end of the long pier, bringing visitors from London. She noticed professional families, white-collar workers and tradesmen on the promenade, all dressed in their Sunday best.

On the shingle beach, people were taking the waters or swimming from bathing huts. Ladies were sitting reading novels, or sewing, while the men read newspapers or looked out to sea through telescopes. Children in sailor suits, frilled bathing costumes and big straw hats, dug holes with their wooden spades, collected shells or paddled with their nursemaids in the shallows. Boats for hire took the more adventurous on sea trips, and horse and donkey carts offered drives and excursions into the surrounding countryside. Less well- dressed people looked as if they had come down for the day to enjoy a glorious brief summer break. Everywhere there were happy faces, excited chatter and laughter.

Turning into Canterbury Road, Bertha found the address she was looking for; a large red brick house with Oaklands Nursing Home on a board at the front. Inside were soft carpets and gay chintzes, a world away from the austerity of the training hospital. Bertha felt suddenly ill at ease in this opulent atmosphere. The matron, wearing a white cap tied under her chin and dark blue dress, showed her into her office to outline her duties.

"We have patients here," she said in her carefully modulated voice, "ranging from the aristocracy to prosperous middle class people. The doctor encourages the patients to take the air and medicinal sea bathes, so you will take patients out to the front in their wheelchairs and the fitter ones to the bathing machines and hand them over to the attendants every day."

The work wasn't as hard nor the rules as strict as at the hospital in London, for this was a sophisticated establishment for genteel patients, who Bertha considered often had little wrong with their health in reality but had been recommended by their doctors to take the sea air as a tonic. There was a well-equipped theatre on the top floor of the building and she noticed that some patients were enjoying a prolonged convalescence from minor operations. Their bedrooms were luxuriously furnished.

There were four other nurses, all a lot older than Bertha. Years of sycophantic nursing had frayed their professional values. In the duty room, a set of numbered bells hung on the wall to summon them at the need, or sometimes, whim of the patients. Usually two or three nurses sat around knitting, chatting or writing letters.

Bertha was shocked when they told her, "You've fallen on your feet here. And you can count on a generous present when the patients leave."

"What – they give you money?"

"Oh no – that would be demeaning - exotic perfume, jewellery, things like that."

"Surely that's unprofessional." Bertha felt like a traitor to all the nurses she had trained with and the ideals of selfless duty she had been taught.

"Oh, well, if you feel like that…you don't have to take it if you don't want."

Bertha felt that she wasn't going to fit in very well here, but next day she met Edith, one of her patients, who suffered terrible "nerves. "Edith told Bertha her story

"I saw Gerald, my fiancé, drowning in the sea. Our families had come down here for a holiday. He went in for a swim and, and…" she broke down in tears and Bertha put her arm around her.

Slowly, day by day, Bertha helped to restore Edith's confidence and heal her broken heart with reassuring cheerfulness and understanding compassion. When Edith's parents came to collect her, they were so pleased with Bertha's good care for their daughter that they gave her a gold brooch. Bertha was embarrassed.

"No, please, I can't take it."

"But you must, Nurse, you've done so much for her – as a token of our gratitude, please. We'll be very hurt if you don't."

Bertha relented, but she still felt it was wrong, to get a present just for doing her job.

On her days off, Bertha was able to explore Herne Bay further; there had been a windmill there once she learned. She saw an old picture and was reminded of the Mill at Tunstall near her home in Suffolk. Her older sister, Rose had sent her a postcard of it - she was now married to the wheelwright's son in Tunstall and had a son. She wrote "Little Willie, sends love and kisses to his beloved aunt Bertha, and thanks her for the chocolates."

Eliza also heard that Bertha was living in Herne Bay and tried to persuade Henry to move down there to be near her. As their daughter, Hilda Rose, had died of scarlet fever, she yearned even more to be united with her lost child.

"I understand why you want to go," said Henry, putting his arm around her. "She's yours, isn't she?"

"What do you mean?" said Eliza, looking away in alarm, "She's my sister, you know she is."

"I've put two and two together about you having the baby all along, love. You forget, I worked at De Vere Hall - people will gossip. The Baron's son - that chap on the horse that day when we watched the Militia go by – that was 'im, wasn't it?"

"Oh, Henry, and you don't mind?"

"I was just waiting till the day you trusted me

enough to tell me. Any child of yours is a child of mine, you silly girl. And I didn't know if you still loved him. After all I'm not much of a catch compared to him."

"You're twice the man he is, Henry. It's such a relief to tell you." She broke down in tears at this and Henry hugged her tight and kissed her and dried her tears.

So Henry found a job and house down in Herne Bay and they moved in.

It was time to tell Bertha about the past too. She had a great need to free herself of the deception of seventeen years. She wanted to tell her the truth now that the girl was grown-up – what had happened between her and Freddie. How much they had loved and lost. So that Bertha would know who her real family were. They arranged to meet in her new home. She was nervous when the time came. How to break the news to her?

"Bertha, how lovely you look! What a fine lady you've become, and a trained nurse too, I'm so proud of you! Sit down by me. Tell me all about it. You know, I wanted to be a teacher when I was at school, but we didn't have the money – I'm so glad you got the opportunity to study."

They chatted happily for a while, then Eliza said, "I have something important to tell you. You know that we all love you very much and …there's no easy way to say this, so I'll just come out and say it…Mother and Father… I know they treated you well…"

"Yes, of course. What is it? What's happened?" Bertha stared at her.

"Nothing's wrong" said Eliza, "not exactly, but it was good of them to bring you up. You see, I gave birth to you, but I was alone. Your father couldn't marry me. So, well, they're your grandparents really. It's me that's your real mother."

"What?" Bertha's face drained of all colour. Momentarily she stopped breathing. This changed everything. Her world fell apart.

"Oh, but I knew it. I knew all along there was something different about me." She sank back in her chair. Eliza tried to put her arms around her but Bertha shrugged her off.

"My darling girl. Don't turn away. You don't know how I've longed for this moment - to have you in my arms as my daughter at last! I never stopped loving you, praying for you, thinking about you."

"You all lied to me. Everyone knew but me. You deceived me!"

"We wanted to protect you. It was done out of love for you. I had to pretend that you were my sister to protect you, to give you a better life. Please forgive me?"

"But who is my father? Why didn't you marry him?"

"Well, we wanted to. Freddie and I were going to run away together but they found out and stopped us."

"Who's they?"

"The De Veres."

"You mean Frederick De Vere – the new Lord De Vere is my father?"

"Yes. That's why they took so much interest in you. They took responsibility for you. They paid maintenance for your upkeep. I was working there as a maid and the young master and I….."

"He seduced you and I was a mistake."

"No, we fell in love and we wanted you, but the Housekeeper found out I was pregnant and sacked me. We were going to run away together but the Baron forbade Frederick to marry me. Mother sent me away to the workhouse where you were born. I had to leave you with Mother and Cecilia made me promise never see him again. I was sworn to secrecy. Everyone said it was for the best. They gave me no choice. Oh, it was terrible. I felt so guilty, so miserable. Please forgive me, Bertha."

Eliza began to cry. She fell onto her knees at Bertha's feet. Bertha pulled her up and hugged her.

"Eliza, I don't blame you. But you must give me time to take this all in. Don't cry -everything has worked out alright in the end. I've been happy. It wasn't your fault."

Walking back to the nursing home thinking about all this, Bertha suddenly felt elated. Such a father! She felt special and proud. But why hadn't Frederick shown more affection towards her? Perhaps if she'd been a boy, or if he had been able to acknowledge her as his daughter, it might have been different, but he seemed content to leave her to his sister, Cecilia.

Finally the mist of half- truths and secrets which had sometimes cast a shadow over her childhood and confused her was cleared away. Many things had puzzled her. Now she had the answers. The last pieces of the jigsaw puzzle to complete the picture of herself. She felt whole. But in the days that followed she still felt a jumble of emotions – anger towards the De Veres, rejection by the big house, and grief for a life that might have been.

In this pensive mood, one day, she wandered alone to Reculver Towers nearby, the remains of a twelfth century Saxon church. Now only the towers and parts of the walls remained as the cliffs were being gradually eroded by the sea and the ruins were right on the edge, with the waves crashing below. The towers were preserved as an important landmark to sailors. She realized that she had been saved by her family and supported by the De Veres.

On her wonderings, she learnt that Herne Bay had originally been a small village with an inn, which was still there. Then a group of businessmen recognised the town's potential as a seaside resort. They built the pleasure pier and promenade, houses and hotels. Steamers stopped there on the way to Margate, bringing holiday- makers.

The truth of her birth lay buried within her. She vowed to herself that she would never disclose the secret to a living soul and would take the truth to her grave. When asked about her father, she would reply, "He was a farmer in Suffolk" and leave it at that.

The De Vere family could never openly acknowledge her. She'd always had the suspicion that her sister Eliza was more to her than a sister, and now she was determined to make her own life a success. She felt driven to excel in her career, to overcome her social disadvantages and forge a place for herself.

Because she had had to learn to live in two very different worlds - the world of an all-powerful father, and the world of his lowly housemaid, as a girl growing into womanhood, the normal problems of finding her own identity were worse for her. She loved books, art, fine furniture, style and fashion and felt a longing to take her rightful place in society - but where exactly was that?

She felt different from other people, an outsider - her high birth, her privileged childhood, the loss she had suffered - she kept to herself. Her past - the mother who could never acknowledge her openly, the father who preferred to keep his identity a mystery - all this had to be kept shut away, a guilty secret - to protect them all from a society quick to condemn. No one must know the truth – that she was illegitimate, born in a workhouse to a servant, but also the natural daughter, the love-child of a Lord, friend of the King.

She'd received a good education and training but now she was an adult and must make her own way in the world - there would be no further contact with the De Veres. She had heard that the old Baron was dead and Cecilia had moved away - it was all in the past, and yet she remembered. Now her real father was Baron and head of the house and estate.

The De Vere estate was a magnet for her when she visited her grandparents, now in their seventies. There she could gaze at the house and gardens, the park, the stables, the home farm and dairy where had she spent much of her childhood, and be grateful. She felt a kind of deja-vue in these places, like a forgotten dream only partly recalled - did it really happen or did she only dream it? The fine furnishings, paintings, library, horses had given her a keen sense of what life was like on the other side of the wealth/poverty divide. She had made the transition from one to the other easily as a child. But where was her place in society now she was grown up? Was she an aristocrat or a lowly villager?

She remembered her benefactors, whose reputation would be ruined if Frederick's indiscretions were known. She didn't want to blacken their name - it was her name too, by rights and yet she was just a servant's child, she didn't have any legitimate claim on the family. But she had been allowed to play at the hall with the other children. She had ridden their horses. Her earliest memories were of the lady who visited her and named her - who treated her as part of the family. Returning to her roots brought back so many memories.... Now she could look back and assess objectively - choose between the values of her village home and what she had been taught at the Hall.

She told her grandmother at the cottage, "I've got mixed feelings about the De Veres. They exploited Eliza, and brought her down and I hate them for that, but they've been generous and kind to me. They tried to make amends and I forgive them."

"She's told you then. Eliza should never have done...what she did. I warned her not to be flighty and behave herself afore she went up there."

"Oh, Mother, it's hard to be good when you are beautiful and men tempt you."

"Beauty's only skin deep. Handsome is as handsome does, I say. And what they did for you was just part of your birthright. It was a lot of trouble and expense for us at our time of life. But we brought you up like our own. We kept your feet on the ground. They spoilt you up there."

Bertha still struggled to deal with the fact that she was illegitimate. Did it mean she was a bad person with low morals? Her mind rebelled at this. Eliza had married and been a good wife and mother all these years. Surely she was an innocent victim, like herself? What she was, what she could be, was up to her alone. I belong somewhere in the middle class, she thought, more cheerfully.

As she slipped inside the De Vere Hall gates, hoping to pass unobserved, like a trespasser, the lodge keeper came out and touched his hat to her,

"Why it's Miss Bertha come back. We heard you was doing nursing in London."

She smiled at the old man, "Just here on a visit, Ted," she said, avoiding his piercing blue eyes. "May I see the garden?"

"Of course you can. His Lordship's up in town but you'll want to see the horses, I suppose. Most of them have been sold. We still got old Blackie, though. He's in retirement now, of course."

She wandered away into the garden and noticed that the old swing was still there, where she used to play so long ago, with the others. She could picture it clearly in her mind's eye - hide and seek among the trees, laughing when the boys found her. The maid walking slowly across the lawn, carrying a tray with glasses of milk....

"Are you going up to the house, Miss?" the voice of the old man interrupted her thoughts,

"No, I don't know any one there now," she replied "Anyway, thankyou Ted, but I've got to get back - I'm on duty tomorrow." She smiled at him.

Then she walked purposefully away, with a wave of her hand, not looking back, that part of her life was over. The next part was about to begin.

20630596R00120

Printed in Poland
by Amazon Fulfillment
Poland Sp. z o.o., Wrocław